1

NEANDERTHAL

1

The Beast Within

by

Vernon Gillen

All of Vernon's book are available at Amazon.com

ISBN - #

978-1720554035

To The Reader

After reading some of my novels people ask if I really am a Christian. Yes I am. However; most people on this Earth are not and they use foul language when they talk. In other words their language has a lot to be desired.

In all of my novels I try to be as realistic as possible. Therefore; some of the characters in my novels use foul language. I apologize for this but it is only a part of my trying to be realistic. I hope that you can overlook these "Imperfections" and still enjoy my novels.

Vernon Gillen

Contents

Chapter I

The Beast

"He was big." a man told the reporter. "I mean he was only about six, six tall but close to three; maybe three and a half feet wide." the man thought for a moment and added; "he did not look … human."

"What do you mean he did not look human?" the reporter asked.

"I saw him earlier and he had a well trimmed beard but this thing had a … scraggily beard. It was thin enough to see the face but the hair. It was about four to five inches long."

"What did you mean by this thing?"

The man looked into the eyes of the reporter and said; "He looked like a Neanderthal … a big caveman."

"That is what everyone here is saying." the reporter said into the camera of the local TV news station. "A man slapped his wife and this man … or thing stood and killed the man … ripping his throat out with his teeth. Then he … or it … let out a yell that some say sounded like a Bigfoot before running out of the restaurant." The reported smiled and continued. "Well I'm sure this Bigfoot did not walk in here to eat fried catfish so where did it come from? Did a man change into this thing when he saw the woman getting slapped? Is the Hulk in town and I was not told?"

The reporter sliced her hand across her throat telling the cameraman to stop filming. Then she and her cameraman went back out to their van and got in and left. The dead man was put in a body bag and carried out to a waiting vehicle. The police could not get a clear story as to what happened. All they knew was what everyone was saying. A man slapped his wife and then another man; or something else, stood and killed the man. After picking the man up into the air this creature that looked like a Neanderthal bit a chunk from the man's throat and then dropped him. After yelling very loudly he or it ran out of the restaurant and vanished into the darkness of the night.

Later that night Michael Gibbins woke up laying in the tall weeds far from the restaurant. When he saw where he was he knew that it had happened again. As usual he remembered what happened.

Young Michael was the son of a well-to-do construction company owner and home maker. Michael had everything he needed and much of what he wanted. His father took him on weekend hunting and fishing trips year round so, that became a big part of his life. And yet; with all that Michael learned about surviving it did not help much with what the world could threw at him. It did not help with what his own government did to him.

Michael made his way back to the restaurant and climbed into his pickup truck. It was already daylight so everyone that had been at the restaurant the night before were gone. It only took Michael thirty minutes to get home but, as he pulled into his driveway he saw the military Humvee and two dully trucks with soldiers in the back. As he got out of his truck a young Private First Class got out of the Humvee.

"You were a bad boy last night Mister Gibbins." the Private said.

"How do you guys know every time I change into … that thing?" Michael asked.

"I don't know … but the Major can tell you I'm sure."

The Private allowed Michael to take his things into his home and lock the home up. Then Michael climbed into the back of one of the trucks and they were off. A few hours later the Humvee and two trucks pulled into Fort Hood and drove to the back of the base where they stopped at a large warehouse.

The truck sat there as the soldiers climbed out and stood in formation. Michael knew the drill and what to do. This was the fourth time that the military found him after he changed and did some kind of destruction. However; this was only the second time he killed a man.

"Okay Mister Gibbins." Private Bails said. "The Major wants to see you again."

Michael climbed out of the back of the truck. He fallowed the Private down the same hallways that he had walked three other times. Finally they got to an office at the back of the warehouse. It was Major Dillard's office.

"There's my man." the Major said as he stood up behind his desk. He stuck out his hand and shook Michael's. Then he offered the chair in front of his desk to Michael and then sat in his chair behind the desk. "So you killed another man."

"He slapped a woman. I just defended her." Michael said.

"Oh I probably would have killed the bastard too but ... we cannot have you changing in the public's eye."

"I know." Michael confessed.

"Now Mister Gibbins ... you're the only one that can control your changing. That's why we allow you to run free. You just need to not do it in public."

"You allow me to run free so you can study me."

"That's true." Major Dillard admitted. "How else can we learn what you all act like?"

"You all." Michael said. "You promised to tell me about the others some day. Well ... I'm not talking anymore until you answer my questions."

The Major waved the two guards out of the office and had Private Bails stay. "Private. Just how bad is your hearing right now?"

Private Bails thought for a moment and then replied; "Really bad Sir. I can't hardly hear a thing."

"You might want to have that checked later but for now just stand there."

"Yes Sir." the Private said.

"Have you ever heard of the Hulk?" the Major asked Michael.

"Yes Sir. There are movies and even a TV show about him." Michael said.

"Well ... he is a real person but ... one of you."

"What do you mean?" Michael asked.

"Back in the 1940's he got out and the public saw him. We could not stop the stories going around so we diluted the story … like we do with stories of UFO's. You see Michael … the Hulk did not really change because of radiation. He changed because he had to many … DNA shots."

"What do you mean? Michael was more confused now than ever.

When you were a child you were among a few of the kids at your school that did not get a TB test but alien DNA injections. Then in the Navy you were being tested for how radiation affected your sperm count. Without knowing that you had alien DNA in you … you were given at that time Neanderthal DNA. It took a few years but you started changing."

So … I'm really a monster?" Michael asked.

"No! Not at all." the Major replied. "You're still Michael Gibbins but … you just cannot get real mad. We have noticed that you can get a little mad but that is all."

"In the movies the Hulk can get shot and the bullets bounce off of him." Michael said just short of the Major interrupting him.

"Oh no. A bullet can kill you after you change just as easily as it can now. That was just one of our diluting stories on the Hulk." the Major said. "We do think that you would instantly heal up when you changed back … we think."

"How do you find me so quickly after I change?" Michael asked.

"We have a satellite up there in space doing nothing but watching you." the Major said with a big smile. "We call it The Gibbinlite. It watches you twenty four hours a day and seven days a week. It can tell us the color of your eyes when you're in a building. I can get the film of what you did in that restaurant last night. It's pretty impressive."

"I heard about the satellite but didn't believe it." Michael sat there knowing that there was no getting away from being watched all of the time. But after killing his second man what

10

was to happen to him now? "So what happens to me now?" he asked the Major.

"I'm not sure but we cannot take you home yet; I know that." the Major said.

"What do you mean?" Michael asked.

"You'll be free to roam the building but that is all for now." the Major suggested. "I think I'll have someone talk to you about controlling your anger. Then we'll take you home."

"And what if I decide to leave?" Michael asked with a smile.

"Remember that bullets would stop you just as they would right now." the Major advised him. "Also … remember when you had that sinus operation a few years back?"

"Yeah!" Michael replied.

"We took advantage of that operation and placed a tiny chip in your brain. We can find you any time we want with that chip."

"That was when those men in black suits came in the operating room."

"That's right." the Major admitted. "The Private will take you to your usual cell but he will leave the door open. You can lay down for a while but I hope to see you at lunch. They are having hamburgers today and their onion rings are to kill for."

"If the Private will wake me I'll be there. Hamburger is about the only beef I eat."

Private Bails lead Michael to the cell that he had been in three other times. As he lay down on the cot the Private left with two soldiers standing guard.

"You two think you can stop me with those M-16s?" Michael asked trying to see if they even knew that bullets would kill him.

"We are here to stop anyone from talking to you Sir." one of the soldiers said. "We don't even know why you're here … just that you're an important person and we have orders to protect you."

"Thanks guys. Get me up for lunch will you?"

"Yes Sir." the soldier said.

Michael lay there thinking about all that he had just learned. He had been given DNA from two sources; alien and Neanderthal against his will. He felt as if he had been raped. If that was not bad enough he was being watched by a satellite all of the time and a chip in his brain kept him from hiding. The depression that he had lived with for so many years just got worse. Michael fell asleep. He had been awake since the morning of the day before. Except for a little sleep in the field before waking up he had, had no sleep.

Just before noon one of the soldiers at Michael's cell woke him up for lunch. He got up and the two soldier fallowed him to the lunchroom in the building. The lunchroom was a small room that had been set up to serve lunches to those that worked there. The food was cooked at the main mess hall on the base and brought there.

As Michael looked down he saw all of the fixings for hamburgers. He always wondered why they were called ham burgers. There was no pork in the meat. Maybe beef burgers did not sound as good as hamburgers. He picked up a plate. The first choice was white or whole wheat buns. He got two of the wheat. Then was the mustard and mayonnaise in squirt bottles and meat patties. After that was lettuce, sliced onions, pickle relish and sliced pickles. Then came the onion rings or French fries that the Major bragged about so much.

As Michael turned he saw the Major waving at him from one of the tables. "I'm happy that you could make it." the Major told Michael. "You can go back for more if you want."

"What actually is your job Major?" Michael asked as he ate one of the onion rings.

"I'm not responsible for what happened to you Michael." the Major assured him. "My job is to monitor you and bring you in when you change in the public's eye. I also clean up the messes you make like what you did last night."

"How do you clean up those … messes?"

"We talk to the people that saw you change and convince them that they did not see anything."

"So you a … threaten them."

"We have to Mister Gibbins." the Major said.

"So if they talk they pop up missing right?" Michael asked.

"Well Mister Gibbins." the Major said. "We have to control the situation and you know … well … what do you think all of those FEMA camps are for? They are for people that refuse to cooperate with their government."

"Is that where I could be heading?"

"Oh no way." the Major said with a big smile. "You would just get mad and break out of there. But if you cannot stop changing in view of the public we will have to confine you someplace … probably with the others."

"You did not explain to much about the others."

"Well …" the Major said as he thought. "Let's just say that they cannot control their changing so we have them locked up where they cannot get away from us. Like you they can be shot and killed but we do not want to do that. There are six others … including the one you call The Hulk. He used to be able to control his changing like you do. But when he could no longer control it we had to lock him up with the others. This is why it is so important that you control your changing. That means you need to learn to control your anger."

"I understand Sir." Michael told the Major. He knew that the Major was right and that he had to start controlling his anger. Only in that way could he control his changing. Then he had another question for the Major.

"What do I actually change into?"

We have three pictures of you after changing that we took from those that took the pictures. Two of these were at the restaurant two night ago. You look like a six and a half foot tall Neanderthal. That must come from the Neanderthal DNA that you were given. We think you may have some traits from the alien DNA but we have not seen it yet."

Michael finished his burgers and onion rings. He was taken back to his cell where he lay down again. Then one of the soldiers mentioned a TV lounge so Michael got up and they lead him there. Michael sat there watch war movies for a while. He saw the ending of Green Berets with John Wayne and then

D Day. While he was watching D Day a woman in a white robe came to him.

"Are you Mister Gibbins?" she politely asked.

"Yes Ma'am."

"If you can fallow me then we can talk and then I think they will be taking you home after that."

"That sounds good." Michael said.

Michael fallowed the woman to her office. She sat in her chair behind her desk and Michael sat in the chair in front of her desk.

"I am Doctor Reilly." she said as she looked through some papers that she pulled out of a file. "Oh I see exactly who you are now."

"Just who am I?" Michael asked.

Doctor Reilly continued to look through the file and then said; "You're one of our guests."

"So that's all?" Michael asked. "I'm just a guest?"

"I have not read your entire file Mister Gibbins but I will. I have been assigned to you to asses your … problem."

"And what problem is that Doc?"

The doctor smiled and said; I know what you change into but your problem, which I will try to help you with, is anger. Evidentially you change when you get angry. So I need to teach you how to control your anger."

"And how are we going to do that?" Michaels asked.

"First I need you to close your eyes."

"I've seen a sex movie that started like this." Michael said with a smile as he closed his eyes.

"I'm married Mister Gibbins so that will never happen."

"I know." Michael said. "I joke to much."

Well lets practice by trying to keep those jokes to yourself."

"Yes Ma'am." Michael said not seeing that the doctor was smiling. In fact she was not even married but was trying to stop any advances that Michael might try.

Now picture in your mind you lifting off of the ground. Now turn around and look down and see yourself still sitting in the chair. Float backwards through the roof of this building. Keep floating to just above the trees. Can you see yourself looking around the base?"

"Yes I ..." he suddenly stopped and opened his eyes. "I was doing fine until I answered you. Then I was back here."

"Perfect. That's what should happen." the Doctor advised Michael. "Your mind has to stay clear. I want you to practice this from time to time. Practice lifting up around another place that you like ... maybe the lake or someplace else."

"That was neat." Michael said.

"Just keep trying this and then you can use it to stop getting so mad."

"Yes Ma'am." Michael said.

The soldiers took Michael back to the TV lounge where he sat down and continued to watch his movies. Then he turned the channel to Fox News. "Oh that's much better." he said as he sank back into the soft couch. A few minutes later Private Bails came and got him. The Private with two soldiers in tow went to the Major's office.

"What'a Go home?" The Major asked Michael.

"Yes Sir. I might like that." Michael answered.

"We'll be taking you home tomorrow morning. Sorry but I cannot get you transportation until then. But we are having baked potatoes for dinner tonight with all of the fixings so you might like that.

"I love baked potatoes Sir."

"I know. That's why I had the mess hall make a few of them for all of us." Then the Major leaned over the desk and whispered to Michael. "I can do that every now and then. I love'em too."

"I'm looking forward to supper then." Michael said.

"That's right. You people out in the country call dinner ... supper."

"Yes Sir but I am getting used to calling it dinner now."

"Oh it's okay." the Major said. "It's just a matter of where you were raised.

Michael was about to get up when the Major stopped him.

"You do know that you cannot go back to that restaurant again don't you?"

"Yes Sir."

Michael went back to the TV lounge with the two soldiers close behind him. It was something that the had gotten used to. He knew that the Major was not going to put up with him changing into this Neanderthal in the public's eye much more. He loved his freedom but if he did not start controlling his anger then he could loose it. As he sat in the TV lounge the doctor came to see him.

"You do not live but a couple of hours from here so I got permission for you to come back and see me about anything that might help you." Doctor Reilly said. Here is my cell phone number in case you need me at night." she said as she handed a piece of paper with her phone number on it." What Michael did not know was that Reilly had more of an interest in him than just her job.

Doctor Evelyn was just two years younger than Michael. Although she had a thriving medical future she was lonely. She did not date and the only place she went outside of the base for her job was church every Sunday morning. She read Michael's file and knew what he was; what he changed into when he got angry but there was still that something about him that drew her to him. She had to get to know this man that she could not get out of her mind.

She watched as Michael stood and put her phone number in his wallet. She was pretty so why not. Before leaving she reminded him that she was really single. That was when Michael realized the reasoning behind her giving him her phone number.

When it was time for dinner Michael went back to the lunchroom. The Major was not there. He picked out the biggest potato that he could see and cut it open with a plastic knife. Then he loaded it with butter; real butter not the artificial type. On top of the butter he added sour cream, chives, and of course bacon bits. After grabbing a plastic glass of tea he sat down. At that time the Major walked in and got what he

16

wanted to eat. Then he sat just across the table from Michael.

"I need to talk with you before you leave." The Major told Michael.

"What's the rush?" Michael asked.

"I guess you don't know yet but ... I got that ride for you tonight. I want you to be taken home in the dark. I have a limo for you so you will not be going backing a military truck. That draws attention and we do not want that."

The Major continued to eat and talk to Michael. Then he gave Michael an ID card so he could get through the main gate.

"It looks like my old military ID card." he told the Major. "I'm not back in the military am I?" he asked as a joke.

"Actually ... you are ... in a way. Face it Michael. Because of what you can change into you belong to the US government. So you might not be a soldier but you still belong to the government like a soldier. Use this card if you need to come back to talk to the Doctor again."

"Yes Sir ... but I doubt if I'll be wanting to come back here."

"The option is there if you need it." the Major advised Michael. "When you finish eating the Private will take you to the car. Just try to control that anger of yours."

Where will you go now?" Michael asked.

Oh that's right. I haven't told you." the Major said as he swallowed what he had in his mouth. "I've been transferred here so I will be here as long as you're alive I guess. I've also be promoted to Colonel thanks to you."

"Well good for you but how did I have anything to do with it?"

"Evidentially; I have been cleaning up the messes you make so well that they want me to stay close to you. I guess that's why I got the promotion as well."

"So you will only be watching me from now on." Michael said.

No ... I will be watching you and one other. He is about to be released as well. He's been doing very well at controlling his temper so we are allowing him to go free."

17

"Who is he? Where will he live?" Michael asked.

"Can't tell you that or anything about him." the Colonel said. "You two are not to meet. He does not even know about you."

After eating Michael and the Private walked to the car which was waiting on him. "By the way. Thanks."

"For what?" Michael asked.

"Thanks to you I am now a Sergeant." Bails said. "I now have six men working under me including the driver ... and them." Bails pointed at two soldiers climbing into the car with them. They carried pistols but no rifles.

Michael sat back in the seat and fell asleep again. When he woke up Bails was waking him up. "Your home." he told Michael. "Don't take this the wrong way but ... I hope I don't see you again."

Michael smiled and said; "I understand." Then he stuck out his hand and shook Bails' hand. "Take care of yourself ... my friend."

"You too man." Michael said as he shut the door to the limo.

Michael gave a last wave as the limo drove off and then unlocked his door. He took a bath and went straight to bed. As he tried to fall asleep he thought about all that had happened. He knew that he had to work on his anger or maybe at least work on not changing. Was it possible? Could he stop changing into this Neanderthal that the Colonel mentioned? He had no idea if he could do it but he had to try. There were one more options. He could go on the run like David Banner did in the TV show; "The Incredible Hulk". Thinking about this Michael finally fell asleep.

Chapter 2

The Other Man

Michael woke up during the night to his outside dog barking. He stepped outside with his pistol but saw nothing or no one. He stepped back into the shadows and stood there for a while. After still seeing nothing moving he went back inside.

Michael went back to bed but could not fall asleep. He wondered if Doctor Reilly really meant what she offered about him calling her. One thing was for sure. He would not mind seeing her again. However; he would wait until later in the morning before calling her.

Unable to sleep Michael got up and turned on his TV. Then he made a pot of coffee as he listened to Fox News on the TV. He usually drank cold coffee in the summer by making it the day and putting the pot in the refrigerator overnight. He had not been there for a couple of days so he had to drink it hot.

After the coffee was made he poured himself a mug and sat on the couch. Then he settled down to drink his coffee and watch Fox News on the TV. Sometime between news about Little Rocket Man in North Korea and the fighting in Afghanistan he fell asleep again.

Michael had a dream about finding the other man that Colonel Dillard had mentioned. The dream did not seem to last long but when he woke up it was already daylight. The sun had not yet come up but he could see around outside. In the cool of the morning Michael got another mug of coffee and went outside. There he sat in his chair overlooking part of his land.

When it started getting warm Michael went back inside. He noticed that it was just after nine in the morning. He decided to call Doctor Reilly. The phone rang five times and he was about to hang up when he heard a voice saying; "Doctor Reilly."

"Ha Doc." Michael said unable to think of anything else to say.

"Who is this?" Reilly asked.

"It's Michael Gibbins." he said.

"Oh Michael. How are you doing?"

"I'm okay I guess but I have been thinking about you ever since I last saw you."

"Now why would you be thinking about me?" the doctor asked being happy that he did call.

"This has nothing to do with you being my doctor but ... how can I ask this?"

"Well what is it about?" Reilly asked.

"It's a personal matter." Michael said. "I remember you telling me when you handed your phone number to me that you were not really married."

"I remember." she said smiling from ear to ear.

"Why did you tell me that?" Michael asked.

"Well ... I was hoping that you might call me sometime." she said.

"As one of your freaks needing help?"

"Not at all ... and you are not a freak." she assured him. "I was hoping that ... sometime you ... might ask me out."

"So I was right. You do want to go out with me right?" Michael was happy.

"Yes."

"What would Colonel Dillard say about that?"

"Well Michael ..." she said and stopped to think about what she was about to say. "... I wouldn't tell him ... and if you had to come here we could not allow anyone to think that we are seeing each other."

"Knowing what I become ... why would you want to date me?" he asked her.

"I really don't know. I liked you ever since I first laid eyes on you." she told him.

"Wow!" Michael said. "I've never been told that before."

Evelyn, or Evie as her friends called her, was a beautiful woman with a perfect figure. She was a little big in the hips but

Michael liked that. She had blond hair and blue eyes and she was just two years younger than Michael. Michael, on the other hand, was almost six feet tall and weighed about two hundred eighty pounds. He had a gut and did not consider himself very attractive. This was why he was wondering why this beautiful woman wanted to date him.

The two continued to talk on the phone for about an hour. Finally they agreed to meet at a Walmart and go out together from there. Michael was excited about the date but so was Evie.

What the two did not know was that their conversation was being listened to. Fort Hood had a program set up where all conversations on the base phones were monitored. Just recently this even included cell phones of those working there. With terrorism getting worse throughout the country this program was a must. Everyone on the base knew that the base phones were monitored but not their cell phones.

"What should we do Sir?" Lieutenant Yoi asked Colonel Dillard.

"Don't let them know that you're listening in on their phones." Colonel Dillard said to the man monitoring the doctor's phone. "Tap his phone as well. We'll just let them date for a while and hopefully they will get closer. Then I'll talk to the Doctor."

That Saturday evening Michael and Evie met at the Walmart parking lot close to the gasoline pumps. From there they went to a local Chinese restaurant and had dinner. As the two sat down to eat Michael reached across the table and grabbed Evie's hand. Not sure what he was doing she looked up at him and saw that his head was bowed.

"Father ... I thank you for the food that we are about to eat. Please bless it and make it nourishment to our bodies. Amen."

Michael let go of Evie's hand and began to eat. As Evie slowly drew her hand back she looked at Michael. This was a side of him that she did not know. She knew that he was a

Christian but many people say that they are Christians but they are not. Many people really believe that they are Christians but when they die they will not be going to Heaven.

As Michael and Evie ate they talked keeping their voices down so that no one could hear them. Evie had many questions and learned a great deal about him that she did not know. In some cases Michael told her something where Colonel Dillard had told her something else. The question was, did the Colonel give her the wrong information about Michael on purpose or was that information what he really believed to be true?

After eating the two went to the movie theater. They decided to watch, about the tenth remake of the original "Wolf Man". No remake would ever be better than the original Wolf Man. Classic movies are classics for a reason, not just because they are old.

When the movie was over Michael drove Evie back to her car. "I really enjoyed myself tonight." Evie said as they both hugged each other.

"Me too." Michael said not sure what he should do next.

"I did not date you tonight because you are … what you are." Evie assured Michael. "I really wanted to go out with you. I like you Michael."

Michael smiled. "I like you too. Would you like to go out again sometime?"

"Of course." Evie quickly answered. "When?"

"I don't know yet but I will call you." Michael said.

"What kind of work do you do?" Evie asked.

"I don't work. I live off of my inheritance … a few hundred thousand dollars."

"Just how many dollars?" Evie asked. "That is if you don't mind my asking."

"I don't usually tell a woman that I have money because I want them to like me not my money."

"But you know that I already like you."

Michael thought for a moment and then said; "About seven hundred thousand dollars."

"You're worth about three quarters of a million dollars?"

Evie asked.

"A little more but don't tell anyone." Michael begged.

"Then you could … disappear … if you wanted."

"Not really." Michael said. "They have a chip in my brain. They have a satellite that watches me all of the time. I could never hide." Michael looked down knowing that he would never be free. "I'm the Colonel's … pet … for the rest of my life."

"Or I could learn more about that chip and remove it from your head for you." Evie commented.

"I just remembered something that the Colonel said." Michael told Evie. He said that the chip was in my brain."

"In your brain?" Evie was not sure what to think.

"Many years ago I was having an operation on my sinuses when some men dressed in black suits came into the operating room. The Colonel said that the tracking chip was placed deep into my sinuses at that time."

"I would not be able to remove that." Evie said. "But I'll see if I can find someone that can."

"Why is this so important to you?" Michael asked Evie.

"Because it is important to you." Evie replied. "That makes it important to me."

Michael and Evie talked a little longer but mostly about their next meeting. No date was set but they both wanted to see the other again. Finally Michael got brave enough to give Evie a kiss and then she climbed into her car. Michael watched Evie's car disappear off into the distance and then got in his truck and went home. Unknown to the two the satellite that watched Michael watched him and Evie all night. Every move was recorded for the Colonel to go over the next day.

When Evie got home she was singing. She really liked Michael and enjoyed being with him on this date. For some reason she started feeling bad. Something was wrong but she had no idea what it was. It was just a feeling but it chewed at her until she fell asleep.

Michael pulled into his driveway also singing. The song on the radio was "Lost in the 50's"; a song that Michael loved. He made a cup of hot decaffeinated coffee and went out on his front porch. Sitting in his chair he looked up at the stars. It was something that he loved doing. By time he finished his coffee he was sleepy. After taking a shower he went to bed.

The next morning Evie got to work early as usual. She was sitting at her desk when around noon the Colonel came into her office. He gave her a smile and then sat in the chair in front of the desk.

"May I help you Sir?" Evie asked not sure what the Colonel was up to.

"Did you enjoy yourself last night?" Colonel Dillard asked.

"Yes Sir but … how … how did you know what I was doing?"

"Michael has a satellite that watches him all of the time. As we watched him last night we inversely watched you as well." the Colonel advised her.

"You were spying on us?" Evie asked as she got mad. "Who in hell do you think…"

"Shut up doctor." the Colonel yelled. "You work for me and because of that you will watch your mouth. Do you understand me?"

Evie waited a moment before answering as she tried to calm down. "Yes Sir." she said through her teeth.

"You're going to do something for me … Doctor."

"And what is that Sir?" she said even still spoke through her teeth.

"You like Mister Gibbins don't you?"

"I don't see how that is any of your business … Sir."

"Oh but it is." the Colonel advised her. "Mister Gibbins is my responsibility. With my raise in rank I was given orders concerning Mister Gibbins."

"And what orders were you given?"

"I was ordered to study him and you're going to help me."

"And if I refuse?"

"Then you will spend the rest of your life in some FEMA camp." he advised her. "You will simply come up missing and then be replaced a day or so later."

Evie was scared and said nothing. She was almost at the point of crying when the Colonel told her that she had nothing to worry about. He reminded her that she worked for him.

Evie took in a deep breath and let it out as she looked down. "What do you need from me ... Sir?"

Evie was in a spot. She had no choice but to do what the Colonel wanted. But the question remained in her head; what did he want her to do? The Colonel went on to explain how that he just wanted her to continue to see Michael but report back to him after each meeting. Then he reminded her that he would be watching them by satellite but the satellite could not hear what they were saying. He wanted to know everything.

"Why do you need to know what goes on and what we talk about?" Evie asked the Colonel.

The Colonel's attitude changed and he got nasty. "Just fallow orders unless you want to be a permanent resident of that FEMA camp."

"I used to have a lot of respect for you ... Sir ... but I have none right now." Evie said with a mean look on her face.

"I don't care how you feel about me as long as you show respect and do what you're told." the Colonel insisted.

"Yes Sir." Evie said through her teeth. "Is that all Sir?"

The Colonel leaned back in his high back chair and smiled as if he was pleased with himself. "Yes Doctor Reilly. That's all."

"Thank you ... Sir." Evie said trying to show some respect.

"Oh! One more thing." the Colonel said. "When are you two suppose to go out again?"

"Don't know." Evie said. "Just agreed to go out again."

"Okay then." the Colonel said. "Just keep me informed."

"Yes Sir." Evie forced the words out as she stood and left the Colonel's office.

Everything in Evie told her to call Michael and let him know what was going on but she knew that even her cell phone was probably tapped. She remembered that the Colonel said that the satellite that watched Michael could not hear things being said around him but was the Colonel telling her the truth. The technology existed where a satellite could listen to what a person was saying even inside a home but could this satellite do it?

Knowing that her cell phone was probably tapped she still called Michael and talked to him. She would make sure that she said nothing that would let the Colonel know that she was going to tell Michael what was going on. She had to set up another date and talk to Michael face to face.

"Hello." Michael said as he answered his phone.

"Michael." Evie said. "How are you doing?"

"I'm doing great now." he said with a big smile.

"I was wondering when we were getting together again." Evie was not the kind of women that asked the man out on a date but she had to talk with him and this was the only way.

"Well I was thinking ..."Michael said. "Do you like to fish?"

"I love to fish and I bait my own hook and take my own fish off of the hook too." she advised Michael.

"Are you a country girl?" Michael asked as he laughed.

"I was raised on a small farm until I left home for college."

"Wow!" Michael was amazed. "I didn't know that about you. I thought that you were the usual city girl that could not survive if food was given to you."

"Why did you think that about me?"

"I didn't really." Michael tried to explain. "I was describing how that a city girl could never survive any disaster. I am into learning how to survive anything that this world throws at me."

"I would love to get into that too." Evie said. Then she thought about what she said and realized that she really would like to learn how to survive things.

The two finally agreed that she would come out to Michael's land the next Saturday morning. His land was on the lake and the cat-fishing there was great. Saturday morning could not come fast enough for Evie but it was only Thursday and she still had to survive the Colonel for two more days. In order to make the Colonel think that she was doing what he wanted she went to his office. His office door was open so she walked right in.

"Michael and I have a date next Saturday." she told the Colonel. "I'll be going out to his place and we are going fishing."

"Great." the Colonel was pleased. "I am also happy that you are doing what I need done too."

"I fallow orders even without your threats." she assured the Colonel.

"For what is worth ..." the Colonel said as the tone in his voice dropped. "I am sorry about that threat of sending you to a FEMA camp. I am under a great deal of pressure from my superiors and they want results not excuses."

"But Michael is the most cooperative subject you have." Evie said. "Why is he so special?"

The Colonel took in a deep breath and let it out. "Michael ... and another man are the only two that can control when they change. My superiors are looking at this as a possible weapon."

"Are you talking about infecting a whole nation?" Evie asked.

"That would be impossible as both men have had DNA injections. My superiors are thinking about infecting ... through DNA injections ... soldiers that we could send into a country and on cue change and destroy an area."

"Who is this other man?" Evie asked.

"We had to bring him in last night after changing in the public's eye ... again." the Colonel advised her. "But you will never know him. He has his own doctor."

Evie had heard about there being another man like Michael but she did not think that it was true.

"This man might not be going out to be free again like Michael." the Colonel went on. "He does not care to even try to control his changing anymore."

"Well I just came in to tell you about our date Saturday, Sir." Evie said.

"Thank you Doctor." the Colonel told her as she turned

and left the office.

Evie went back to her office and sat behind her desk. She thought about the other man and then realized that the Colonel said that the man was there. There was only a few cells in which to hold the man so she got up to go there.

When Doctor Reilly walked into the area where the cells were the two soldiers standing guard allowed her by. They knew her and thought that she was there doing her job.

"Where is the man they brought in last night?" she asked one of the guards.

"Over here Doctor." the guard pointed at one of the cell doors.

Evie walked up to the cell door and looked through the window. All she could see was a man laying on the cot.

"He's sedated Ma'am." the guard told her. "They had to bring him in that way."

"Who is keeping him sedated?" she asked the guard.

"I thought you were." the guard said as he looked at the other guard. "Are you suppose to be here ma'am?"

"I was told to check on him." Evie lied through her teeth as she left the area. "He seems to be okay."

The next morning when Evie walked into her office she found the Colonel sitting at her desk. As he saw her walk in he got up to let her have her chair.

"You need something Sir?" Evie asked as she sat in her chair.

"I got word that you went to see the other man in his cell yesterday." the Colonel calmly said.

"Yes." she admitted. "And ..."

"And I told you that he had a doctor and it was not you." The Colonel was upset with her.

"You never told me not to go take a look." she tried to defend herself.

"Don't push me Doctor." the Colonel said as he tried to keep the tone of his voice down.

"Sorry Sir." Evie pretended to be submissive. "It won't happen again."

The Colonel smiled and said; "Sounds good to me." Then he left the Doctor's office and her sitting behind her desk.

All Evie could think about was that Saturday morning could not come fast enough. She was not only looking forward to her fishing trip but she had even more to tell Michael now.

Later that evening Evie called Michael and asked when she should be at his place. He told her that the best fishing was just after daylight. She needed to be there before daylight. Joking she asked if she could just go ahead and come there that night and sleep there.

For a moment Michael was quiet. Then he said that she could take his bed and he would sleep on the couch. Evie liked Michael a great deal but she was not yet ready to be sleeping with him. His offer to sleep on the couch helped her to feel better after offering to spend the night. She now worried about how she looked in his eyes.

A woman that will sleep with a man afternoon one date will sleep with anyone that quickly. Then you have to wonder how many diseases that woman might have had when you slept with her. Evie just hoped that she did not look easy and cheap.

Evie took off work early knowing that the Colonel would not care. She went home and packed a few things in a bag and left for Michael's home. All the way to his home she worried about sounding cheap on the phone but also hoping that he did make a move. She was just wanting their first time to be something special. Evie was still a virgin. But just in case the situation came up she did pack a sexy nightgown in her bag. She also packed shorts and a T shirt that she would wear if the situation did not come up.

Chapter 3

Stalker

It was almost dark when Evie pulled into Michael's driveway. She found his home by using her GPS on her cell phone. Before she could get out of her car Michael was at the side of her car. He opened the door for her and she got out. This time they instantly gave each other a hug.

Michael carried Evie's bag into his home and back to the bedroom. When he came out Evie asked if she could take a shower.

"Of course." Michael said. "You will find towels in there."

"Sorry but I just wanted to get out of there." Evie said. Then she added; "… and we need to talk."

"You want some coffee or maybe hot cocoa or hot apple cider when you get out?"

"Apple cider sounds great." Evie told him.

Michael get everything ready for their drinks. He also decided to have a mug of the hot apple cider. As he worked to make things perfect he could hear Evie singing in the shower. He got his mug of cider and sat on the couch. He was watching a western movie but changed the TV to Fox News to see if there was anything new.

A few minutes later he looked to his left and saw Evie walking into the kitchen to get her cup of cider. All she had to do was add the hot water. Then Michael noticed that she was wearing a pare of shorts and a T shirt. As she turned towards him he noticed that she was also wearing a bra under her T shirt.

"Damn." he said to himself.

"Do what?' Evie asked as she walked into the demands down close to Michael.

"Oh nothing." Michael said not realizing that he said it so

loud.

When they both finished their cider they just sat there watching Fox News and talking about what was being said. After a while Michael took a chance.

"I am not one to force myself on a woman but ... if you want to slide over a little closer so I can hold you then I would like that."

She smiled and slid up against him. "I was hoping you would want to hold me."

For hours the two talked as Evie told Michael all that she had seen and heard. He knew about the satellite watching him but did not like them watching him and Evie together.

"Are you sure that the Colonel cannot hear us talking." Michael asked.

"He said that the satellite watching you ... and us right now ... could not listen to us but I know that there are satellites than can. I just don't know if this one can."

But if we whisper into each other's ears ..." Michael suggested.

"Oh I like that idea." Evie said as she slid even closer to Michael. Before long neither of them were paying any attention to what was being said on the TV. They found out that cuddling was something that they both loved doing.

"I need to tell you something Michael." Evie said.

"What is it?" Michael was getting ready for some bad news.

"I'm still a virgin and I want to stay that way."

Michael smiled and said; "I think I can work with that.

The two continued to cuddle and watch the TV for another hour. The couch was not slept on that night but they both got a good night's sleep. The best thing of all was that the next morning Evie woke up still a virgin. Michael was an honorable man and she knew right then that she had to keep him. Good men like this were hard to find and she was not letting this one get away.

The alarm clock went off at 0500 hrs. Michael and Evie got up and got dressed to go fishing. Before Michael could even get his pants on Evie walked around the bed and gave him a big hug.

"Thank you." she said.

"For what?" Michael wondered.

"For keeping your word and not touching me."

Michael smiled and said; "I think we both touched each other allover last night."

"I mean…" Evie was trying to think of a way to say it. "…I'm still a virgin. Thank you for keeping your word."

"Oh is that all." Michael shrugged it off. "Let's go fishing."

For a few moments Evie just stood there and looked at Michael with a big smile. She was starting to like this man a lot more. That night was the most memorable night that she had ever had. Could Michael be the man that she had been looking for. She wondered this while in the back of her hear she also remembered what he became. If they got married and had kids would his DNA effect their children? Now she began to worry.

Michael and Evie went down to where Michael's land went into the lake. He backed up his pick-up truck so they could use the tailgate as a table for baiting hooks and taking catfish off of the hooks. Michael got his cast net and cast it a few times but only caught a few shad for bait. After about fifteen minutes they had enough shad to start fishing. Michael continued to throw the cast net while Evie baited and cast out two poles for her. By then they had plenty of shad to fish with until it got hot.

The catfish were not biting well but the turtles were. Every now and then one of them would catch a catfish big enough to keep. Then Michael finally hooked a big one. Luckily he caught it on his big pole. It and the real were designed to catch bigger fish.

Michael fought the catfish for about ten minutes before bringing it close to the bank. Then he stepped into the water and grabbed the catfish by sticking his four fingers into the gills. It was huge. He pulled the catfish onto the bank and up to the truck. As he worked to take the hook out of the fish's mouth it flounced sending the hook deep into Michael's hand.

Then it flounced again ripping the hook through Michael's hand. Then Michael let out a blood curdling yell from the pain.

Michael began to change as he continued to yell. Suddenly Evie yelled at him causing him to look at her.

"Michael." she yelled trying to get his attention. "I know it hurts but don't change. Hold your hand and concentrate on not being angry."

Michael held his hand. The pain was great but he knew that he had to do what Evie said. She was trying to help him. Suddenly he found Evie in front of him reaching out to hug him.

"There you go." Evie told him. "You're doing it. You're turning back into a human."

Seconds later Michael stood there holding Evie. He was almost back to being normal. However; his hand was still bleeding. As Evie looked at his hand she noticed that it was almost completely healed. She looked up at him and saw that his eyebrows were still over handing like a Neanderthal. She watched his face as it slowly went back to a normal human face. Then she looked at his hand and saw that the wound was healed. There was only a scar.

Michael got weak as he always did after changing back into a human. He climbed into the passenger side of the truck while Evie got all of he fish they caught and the fishing gear loaded in the back of the truck. Then she drove back to Michael's home.

Evie got Michael into his home and then went out to the truck and got the catfish which were on a stringer. After placing the stringer in the rain barrel she went back inside. Michael had passed out on the couch where she left him. She pulled his boots off and turned him around to lay on the couch. She knew that he would wake up soon enough.

Evie went back outside and got the catfish. They had three. She cleaned the catfish and placed the meat in a zip lock bag. When she finished she placed the bag in the freezer. Then she sat in another chair and watch the TV. About thirty minutes later Michael woke up.

Instantly Evie went over to Michael. "You feeling better Baby?"

"Yeah!" he said trying to sit up. ""You okay?"

"Oh yes." Evie answered.

After Michael sat up Evie squeezed in beside him and under his arms. With his arms around her he gave her a tender squeeze assuring her that everything was okay.

"You weren't scared when started to change?" Michael asked.

"At first but I knew that I had to try to get you to stop changing ... and it worked." she said with a big smile.

Michael looked at his hand. "It's healed."

"Yes. I watched it heal as you changed back to human." Evie advised. "Your eye brows were the last thing about you to change back."

"The fish." Michael suddenly said.

"I cleaned them and put them in the freezer." Evie quickly told him.

"You take them home." Michael insisted. "I can get more when ever I want."

"Not if they are biting like they were today." Evie said with a big grin on her face.

Michael and Evie spent the rest of the day cuddling on the couch and watching a few movies. That evening he said that he wished she would spend the night. She agreed. Soon after that Evie went into the restroom and took a shower. This time when she came out she was wearing her sexy nightgown. When she sat on the couch and slid closer to Michael he did not know what to do.

"You're making it real hard for me." he told Evie.

"What do you mean?" she said keeping her head down so he could not see her smiling.

"I know you want to remain a virgin and ..." he said.

Evie moved so that her mouth was close to his ear and whispered; "Maybe I changed my mind."

Michael was quiet for a while. He had no idea as to what he should say. Then finally he asked; "What do you mean?"

34

"I said what I meant to say." Evie continued to whisper. Maybe I don't want to be a virgin anymore."

Michael smiled and asked her; "Want to go in the bedroom and talk about it?"

Evie leaned forward and stretched. "I don't know." she said teasing him.

"I do know." Michael said as he got up and pulled her up as well. Still holding on to her wrist he quickly made his way to the bed. Laying on the bed Michael pulled Evie beside him.

The next morning Evie woke up around 0300 hours. Michael was not in the bed. She got up and found him outside sitting in his chair on the porch. He had his mug of coffee and was staring at the stars.

"You okay Baby." she asked him.

"Come back to bed." she begged.

Michael decided to do some teasing of his own. "But I have already done my duty in there."

Evie got upset. "What do you mean your duty?"

"You did not want to be a virgin anymore and I took care of that." Michael was having fun. "I already did my duty."

After that Evie was mad. "Well don't help me with any more favors."

As Evie started to storm away Michael quickly got up and grabbed her. After wheeling her around he gave her a very passionate kiss. That was all it took to melt her heart.

"You know you're a spoilt brat right?" Michael asked her.

With a big smile on her face she asked; "You want to go back to bed and spoil me some more?"

Michael raised his arms and stretched like she had done the night before. "I guess so. What else is there to do?"

"Well don't do me any favors." Evie said as she started to walk off. Michael was still holding her arm and would not let go. The two went backing the bedroom and stayed until long after the sun was up. That evening Evie had to go home so that she could be at work early the next morning.

Back at Fort Hood Michael and Evie's fun had been observed by satellite and being recorded for the Colonel to view later. A phoned call to the Colonel caused him to come in that Sunday morning.

Well … she's doing what I told her to do." the Colonel said to Lieutenant Rubin.

Lieutenant Rubin was the Head of Satellite Operations at Fort Hood. He was a tall skinny man, about twenty four years old. No one knew it but he had a thing for Doctor Reilly before she even met Michael. Spying on her and Michael was pleasurable to him. He had only asked her out once but she smiled and then turned him down. If he could not have her then he would ruin her reputation. Maybe then she would turn to him.

Lieutenant Rubin was a man that walked that fine line between genius and insanity. Most of the time he was a genius but he sometimes leaned over to the insanity side of he fence. Just three years earlier he had been committed toa mental institution after stalking a women. She said that he kidnapped her and took her to his home where he raped her many times. No evidence was found to back up the woman's story and the psychiatrist released him after only three days.

Rubin was working for Colonel Dillard at the time and some said that the Colonel got the Lieutenant out early. Rubin's being committed was kept a secret. No one at Fort Hood knew about it except Colonel Dillard. Evie did not know it but she was in danger. She had been stalked before by the creepy Lieutenant but she was now being stalked by satellite.

Although Colonel Dillard knew what th Lieutenant had done and even helped him from going to prison he really believed that the Lieutenant had stopped his stalking ways. He had no idea that Lieutenant Rubin just changed who he was stalking.

Being upset with Michael's dating Evie Rubin experimented with Michael's tracking chip. One day as he watched Michael from the satellite he was able to cause a feedback to the chip in Michael's head causing Michael to have pain. By increasing the feedback he was able to cause Michael even more pain. Suddenly he stopped what the Colonel walked into the room.

"Have you learned anything new?" the Colonel asked Lieutenant Rubin.

"No Sir." the Lieutenant said with a smile.

The Colonel looked at Rubin and asked; "Why are you smiling?"

"Oh nothing Sir." Rubin said." They do seem to like their sex." When the Colonel left he room Rubin added; "But I'll see if I can change that." That was when Rubin decided to only use the feedback when Michael and Evie were together.

When Rubin went home that evening he got on his computer and set up a connection from his home computer to the satellite watching Michael. Then he started working on making a connection to the tracking chip in Michael's head. Knowing the frequency of the tracking chip he worked for hours trying to set it in his home computer. Around midnight he completed the connection. Now he was able to watch Michael and mess with the chip in his head from home.

Michael and Evie had been seeing each other on the weekends when Rubin was off duty and at home. The only reason he was able to watch Michael and Evie the Sunday before was because he worked another man's duty shift. Now he could watch them from home. Now he could cause Michael pain whenever he and Evie were together; also from home.

Throughout the next week Rubin did his usual job and pretended to not have much interest in what Michael did. On that Wednesday morning Evie came into the Satellite Room to see what Michael was up to. She had not talked to him since their last date. She had no idea that Rubin was stalking her; and Michael.

"Good morning Rubin." Evie said with her usual smile.

"Good morning Doctor." he replied trying to sound uninterested in her being there.

"How is Michael doing?" Evie asked still smiling.

"He's fishing again." Rubin said not realizing that he had said it in a snobby way.

"You okay Rubin?" Evie asked.

37

"Oh yeah." he quickly thought about how he had to say things. "I just don't like fishing. I don't like anything that involves hurting an animal."

"Well Rubin ..." Evie said trying to be nice about what she was about to say. "Where do you think mean in the store comes from?"

"But that meat is raised on farms for the purpose of being butchered." he replied trying to defend his position on the matter.

"What's the difference?" she asked him.

"Can't Michael just go buy his fish in the store instead of killing the fish from the lake?"

"Some people like the sport." Evie said defending Michael.

"Fishing and hunting should be outlawed." Rubin insisted.

Knowing that she was getting no place with Rubin and his liberal beliefs Evie turned her attention back to Michael. "Is he catching anything?"

"He's murdered a few." Rubin said in a snobby way again.

"Okay Rubin." Evie said trying to defuse this situation. "See you later Rubin."

Now Rubin was mad at Evie. She did not believe things the way he did and therefore did not deserve his love. "I could have given you the world and all of the love in my heart with it." he said to himself. "Now you can suffer with him by watching him suffer."

That night when Rubin got home he quickly went to his computer and connected to the satellite watching Michael. Michael was already back home and was sitting on the couch watching his TV. Rubin reached over to a knob that he turned that increased the feedback on the chip in Michael's head.

First Rubin just barely turned the knob but there was no reaction from Michael. He turned the knob a little more and there was still no reaction. As he continued to turn the knob he continued to see no reaction from Michael. Finally he realized that the knob was not working.

What Rubin did not know was that the battery in Michael's chip had failed and the chip was no longer letting them know where he was. This did cause a little bit of a headache but that was all. Three Ibuprofen relieved the pain but it came back about an hour later. By time Evie drove up to his home Saturday morning he had been in a lot of pain.

When Evie walked into Michael's home she instantly saw that he was in pain. She sat beside him on the couch and noticed that a little blood was coming from his right nostril.

"Come with me Michael." Evie said. "I've got to get you to Fort Hood."

"Why?" he asked half dazed from the pain. "What's wrong?"

"I think your tracking chip is causing you problems." Evie told him.

Evie helped Michael to her car and got him strapped in the passenger seat. The after a quick look around to make sure that no one was watching she got into her car and cranked it up. Then they were on their way to Fort Hood.

Chapter 4

The Chip

It was around noon before Evie drove into Fort Hood. She had already called Colonel Dillard so that he could have things set up and ready when she and Michael got there. As she drove through the gate two Humvees with flashing blue lights took the lead. Evie fallowed them all the way to the back of the base where the large warehouse was. As she pulled up a medical team got Michael and helped him to lay on a gurney.

Michael was wheeled into an operating room but Evie was held outside. "You can't go in ma'am." an armed soldier told her. She knew that he was right and found a set of chairs and sat down. A few minutes later Colonel Dillard walked up and sat beside her.

"What happened?" the Colonel asked Evie.

"I don't know." she said. "I walked into his home and he was sitting on his couch half out of it."

"What do you mean ... half out of it?"

"He looked like he was in another world. He answered some of my questions but I had to help him walk to my car." Evie said as she started to cry.

"You did the right thing ... bringing him here you know."

Evie and the Colonel talked for a long time as she answered every question he had. Then they went to the eating room and got a cup of coffee each.

"What is going to happen to Michael?" Evie asked the Colonel.

"They will remove the tracking chip and check it out."

"And if it is bad?"

"A new one will be put where the other one was." the Colonel sounded so cold about this.

At that time one of the surgeons walked up to the Colonel

with the old tracking chip in his hand. It had been cleaned so the Colonel could handle it.

"I am not an expert on these things but I do know that it is not suppose to be brown. It is suppose to be white."

"Would it turn brown through time?" the colonel asked.

"No Sir. They stay white."

"What could cause it to turn brown?" Evie asked but the surgeon did not answer her.

"I'm sorry Doctor." the Colonel said to the surgeon. "This is Doctor Reilly … that man's doctor. She works here."

"Oh okay." the surgeon said. Then he turned to Evie and said; "It is my guess that only heat could do this." he told Evie. "But like I said … I am not an expert on these things. I just put them in a person when the Colonel orders me to do so."

Evie started thinking that she may have found the person that could remove Michael's chip. The question was; would he do it. She looked at the surgeon's nametag. His name was Tray Wheelhouse. She would look him up later.

"Did you replace this chip with a new one?" Evie asked the surgeon.

"Oh yes ma'am." he quickly answered. "This one has a longer lasting battery."

The surgeon answered a few more of the Colonel's questions and then left. When Evie and the Colonel finished their coffee they went back to the operating area to wait for Michael to come out. By time they got there he had already been moved to one of the cells so they went there.

When Evie passed the cell where the other man had been she looked in through the window. The man was no longer there.

"Where is the man that was in here?" Evie asked the Colonel.

"Like I told you … he did not want to cooperate with us." the Colonel said. A few days ago he turned and tried to escape and got shot for his troubles."

"Did he survive?"

"No Doctor." the Colonel sadly said. "After he killed the

41

third soldier I ordered him to be killed." Then he looked at Evie and added; "This is why I need Michael to stay under control. You may not believe this but I like Michael and I do not want to see him harmed."

"You would have him killed as well?" Evie asked.

"Only if I had to." the Colonel admitted. "We cannot have our ... test subjects running free if they cannot or ... like this man ... will not cooperate with us."

"I understand Sir." Evie admitted.

"You really like him don't you?" the Colonel asked with a smile.

"Yes Sir. Very much."

"Then keep him under control."

That was when Evie told the Colonel about when Michael got that hook in his hand. She had to talk him down but he did stop changing right in the middle of his change. Then he changed back to human form and his hand had healed.

The Colonel was surprised that Michael's hand healed. Only two other subjects were able to do that and they were both being held in a more secure facility under ground in Oklahoma.

Evie was learning a lot with the Colonel's open mouth. She found a surgeon that might remove Michael's tracking chip and she learned that the others like Michael were being held underground someplace in Oklahoma. Those being held underground in Oklahoma were the ones that could not or would not control their changing so she did not care about them. She did care about Michael and was devoted to helping him. She did not know it at that time but she was falling in love with Michael.

Evie looked up to see four armed soldiers standing at the door of the cell in front of her. The Colonel ordered one of the soldiers to unlock the cell door. As the door opened the Colonel and Evie stepped inside.

Michael was laying on a cot but he was starting to come out of his sedation. Evie quickly knelt beside the cot.

"How are you feeling Baby?" she asked Michael.

42

"Better. No headache … now." he said in broken English. Then he reached out and took Evie's hand in his and added; "Missed you."

After that Michael fell asleep again. The Colonel told Evie that Michael was getting the best of care and they needed to leave and let him rest. The Colonel walked Evie to his office where she sat down in the chair in front of the Colonel's desk.

"Is there anything else you need to tell me?" he asked her.

Evie was not about to tell the Colonel everything but still thought about what she might could tell him. "No Sir." she said. "Already told you all I know."

"Then go home and get some rest and … thanks for bringing him here. You might have saved his life."

Evie got up and walked to her office. She looked around to see if there was anything she might want to take home with her but saw nothing. Then she decided to go back to Michael's home. He had two dogs that might need food and water.

By time Evie got to Michael's home it was almost dark. She unlocked the door with the hidden key and went inside. Michael had a Miniature Dotson inside his home named Odie. She checked his food and water and found that he had plenty. Then she checked the outside dog. This dog had a simpler name. His name was Dog.

"Dog." Evie yelled. "Where are you Dog?"

Finally Dog ran up to her and almost knocked her down trying to jump up on her. Both of Michael's dogs like Evie a great deal. She checked Dog's food and water and found that he also had plenty. After giving Dog a little more loving she went back inside.

Evie got herself a mug of apple cider and sat down on the couch. Odie quickly jumped up in her lap but lay down beside her. As she turned the TV on she looked around. To her left was the kitchen. Farther to her left was the master bedroom. In front of her was the TV and on the wall behind it hung many pictures of Michael's family and ancestors. Michael was very proud of his Irish heritage and had even written a book on his bloodline. To the right was another wall of pictures and farther to the right was a hallway that lead to two more bedrooms and a half bath. Behind her was the front door which she made sure was locked after she came in.

Keeping the doors locked was part of that survival thing that she was learning from Michael. She knew one man that used to leave his doors unlocked until one day three men came rushing into his home. They shot him, his wife and two kids. He was the only one that survived. He now keeps the doors to his home locked but; that lesson cost him dearly.

That night Evie slept in Michael's bed. She woke up many times during the night worrying about him. She ended up staying until she went home Sunday evening. Monday morning she was at work early as usual.

The first thing that Evie did when she got to work was check on Michael. He was still asleep so she went to her office. A few minutes later Rubin came into her office.

"Good morning Rubin." Evie politely said.

"What's wrong with your boyfriend?" Rubin asked.

"How did you know…" she said before realizing that he had been watching them. "That right. You do know. He's doing fine I guess."

"You sound like you don't care."

"I checked on him before coming to my office but he was still asleep." she said.

"What was wrong with him?" Rubin asked hoping to find out something about Michael's tracking chip.

"That chip in his head shorted out or something." Evie said not knowing that she was helping Rubin. "They had to replace it."

"Is he going to be okay?" Rubin asked as if he really cared.

"In time he will." Evie admitted. "That's all I know."

"To bad." Rubin whispered to himself.

"To what?" Evie asked not sure what he had said.

"I said to rad." he told her. "The way the kids today talk … to radical. In other words that's good."

"I could not care less how the kids today talk. They're all nuts that think they know everything." she confessed how she

44

felt about today's kids.

Rubin said good by and then left Evie's office. He knew that in a day or so he would be given the frequency to Michael's new chip. It was part of his job. He would wait until then to get it. However; he knew that he had to be more careful. If he burned out another chip it might draw attention and cause an investigation.

Rubin's infatuation with Evie was growing. Sometimes he loved her more than any man could and other times he was so mad he could hurt her. But he thought that, that was what love was all about. He really believed that he was in love with Evie and if he could not have her then no one could have her.

That night Evie went to see Michael. He was already walking around his cell. The Colonel had no reason to think that he might try to run so he ordered the guards to be removed and the cell door left open.

"You're looking better." Evie told Michael.

"I'm feeling better too." Michael advised her. "The surgeon ... Doctor Wheelhouse ... said that he would be releasing me tomorrow morning."

"Great." Evie was excited. "I'll take you home ... that is if you're up to it."

Michael smiled at how she said that but told her that he just wanted to get home. She assured him that Odie and Dog had been taken care of and there was nothing to worry about.

"Thanks for taking care of them Babe." Michael said.

"Wow!" Evie said. "That's the first time you've used a pet name for me. I've been calling you Baby for a while now."

"I'm sorry." Michael admitted. "It has to feel right before I call anyone Babe."

Evie scooted up against Michael and put her arms around him. "I'll let you slide this time."

"Oh you will." he said as he gave her a big smile.

While Michael and Evie continued to hold each other someone was watching them. Rubin was gritting his teeth as he used the satellite to spy on Michael and Evie; mostly Evie. The more he watched them the madder he got.

That night when Evie got home she called Michael. They talked for over an hour. Then Evie had to go so she could get some sleep. She was taking Michael home the next morning.

The next morning when Evie came in she was called to the Colonel's office. He had a few questions for her and then let her go for the day. While she was still in the Colonel's office there was a knock at his door.

"May I speak to you Sir?" a man at the door asked.

As the man walked in he looked at Evie and then the Colonel. "Could we speak alone Colonel?"

"Of course Doctor." the Colonel said. "Take care of my man Doctor Reilly." he told Evie. Evie left and closed the door behind her.

"So Doctor Richards." the Colonel said. "What do you have for me about that chip?"

Doctor Ted Richards worked at Fort Hood under the Colonel. He was the person that designed the tracking chips like the one in Michael's head. He was a thirty eight year old, tall but heavy set man.

"I've been looking at this chip and found that the battery was not the problem." Richards advised the Colonel.

"What do you mean?"

Richards held the chip in his hand. "This little thing gives off a signal at a frequency that the public is not allowed to use. In this way you can track who ever it is in."

"I know that." the Colonel mentioned.

This little baby was sending out that signal when ... for some reason ... that signal was sent back causing what is called a feedback loop. That's what burned it out."

"Do you think it was an accident or did someone do it on purpose?" the Colonel asked.

"Sorry Sir but this could not happen by accident. Someone caused the feedback loop on purpose. For what reason ... I don't know."

"Any idea who could have or even would have wanted to do it?"

"No Sir." Richards replied. "It could have been a kid with

a new drone that he messed with and changed the output frequency. Or it could have been North Korea, China, or Russia."

"Why would a foreign government cause a feedback in these chips?" the Colonel asked.

"There would be no reason for then to do it." Richards said. "The only thing a feedback loop would do is heat the chip up and cause pain in the person that it was in." Richards started to walk out of the room but turned and added; "I suggest that you stop placing these chips in a man's head before you loose an important man. I don't know how this man is still alive. I would put them someplace else."

When Richards opened the door he saw that Evie was standing there. She quickly walked away as if no one had seen her. Richards and the Colonel both knew that she had heard everything.

"I wouldn't worry about her Doctor." the Colonel told Richards. "She is Michael's doctor." He neglected to say that she was also dating Michael. He did not want Richards to worry. On the other hand he would have to talk to her.

Evie and Michael were just about to leave when the Colonel came to see them. "You don't need you to leave yet Michael." he told them. I am sure that Evie told you about the chips. After all … she heard everything from the other side of my office door." The Colonel took a few steps closer and added; "I am not sure that this feedback loop was not caused on purpose."

"What are you saying Colonel?" Michael asked.

"We need to remove that new tracking chip from your head. If this happens again it could kill you." the Colonel advised. "I don't think you need a tracking chip anymore anyway. You've been pretty good about working with me and Doctor Reilly said that you're controlling your changing better too."

"So what do we do now?" Evie asked.

"Michael needs to stay so we can take that thing out in the morning. Since the damage to that area of his brain from the burned chip is healing now you should be able to go home a few hours after removing this chip."

"I guess I can wait one more day." Michael said with a big smile.

"Then I will set it up with Doctor Wheelhouse." he said as he left the cell.

"Well then ... I guess I'll get some work done while I'm here." Evie said.

Evie kissed Michael and then went to her office. That evening she stopped to see him before going home but he was asleep. She let him sleep and went on home. That night she thought about this second person that might be able to remove the chip but there was no need now. The Colonel was not having it placed back in Michael's body someplace else.

The Next morning Doctor Wheelhouse came into the Colonel's office just before operating on Michael. He had a cup of coffee in one hand and papers in the other hand.

"You wanted to see me Sir?" Doctor Wheelhouse asked.

"Yes I did." the Colonel said.

"When you remove that new tracking chip from Michael's head this morning ... where could you put it where he will not find it or where he would not be able to cut it out if he did find it?" the Colonel asked.

"Well Sir ..." the Doctor said as he thought about it. "... I could place it under his arm. He has a few tags in his right armpit. I could remove them and put the chip just under the skin there. Then you could tell him that I removed those tags for him. He will not even know to look for the chip."

"Perfect." the Colonel said with a big smile. "You do that but keep this between us."

"Yes Sir." Doctor Wheelhouse agreed.

Two hours later Evie was sitting just outside the operating room waiting for Michael to come out. Colonel Dillard walked up and asked her if she had heard anything. She said that she had not heard anything yet. A few minutes later Doctor Wheelhouse walked out of the operating room.

Looking right into the Colonel's eyes the Doctor said;

48

"Everything is finished." Then he looked at Evie and added; "He had a few tags under his right arm."

"Yeah but they were not painful. It did bother him to have them though." Evie admitted.

"Well I removed them for him so he will be a little tender there for a while." Wheelhouse told her.

"Thanks." Evie said with a smile. "He'll be happy to know you did that."

Before leaving Wheelhouse looked at the Colonel and told him that Michael could go home when he woke up but he could not drive yet. That was when Evie said that she would be taking him home.

Although Michael woke up less than an hour later it was another two hours before he was able to walk on his own. He was still just to drowsy. Evie walked right beside Michael to help him if he needed it. When they got to her car she helped him into the car and then she climbed into the driver's seat. Three and a half hours later Evie drove into Michael's driveway.

Dog was getting used to Michael climbing out of the passenger side of Evie's car and met him there. When Michael opened the car door Dog tried climbing into Michael's lap. He gave Dog a little loving and that was all he wanted. Evie helped Michael out of her car and into his home where he sat on the couch.

Odie jumped on the couch and into Michael's lap. He tried to lick Michael's face but Michael stopped him. All of this was going on while Evie made some coffee. He felt his right armpit and it was tender just as Doctor Wheelhouse said it would be.

A few minutes later Evie came into the den with two mugs of coffee and sat beside Michael. She turned the TV to Michael's favorite channel; Fox News.

Chapter 5

Last Warning

Michael almost always watched Fox News on his TV. He never watched or listened to what the Liberal/Communist had to say on the local channels. The only time he watched the local news was to get the local weather. Then he would always quickly turn his TV back to Fox News.

Michael also loved watching movies. His favorite were World War Two movies but he also watch anything with Audie Murphy or John Wayne in it. However; his favorite movie was Midway which neither actor played in.

It was hard to put his arms around Evie as she sat on his right side. Spreading out his arms hurt so she just scooted as close to him as she could.

On that morning Lieutenant Rubin received the frequency for Michael's new tracking chip. He was not told that the chip had been relocated to Michael's right armpit. Thinking that the chip was in Michael's head where the other one had been he turned his dial to cause Michael a little pain. Watching Evie scooting closer to Michael enraged Rubin. As he watched the two he wondered why Michael did not have his arm around Evie. Maybe the headache he thought that he was causing was working.

Michael stated feeling a slight burning feeling in his right armpit but he just thought that it was the tiny open cuts from removing the tags. After a while it bothered him enough that he mentioned it to Evie. He raised his arm and Evie looked but only saw the cuts where the tags had been removed. Seeing nothing else he lowered his arm and they continued watching the TV.

When Rubin realized that what he was doing was not stopping Michael and Evie from being with each other he turned down the knob that controlled the tracking device feedback. He did not want to burn this chip out. He also wondered why Evie was looking under Michael's arm. He lived out in the country where people get ticks all of the time. Was she checking an itch he had? It puzzled him but he forgot about it and just went back to doing his job; just watching Michael.

Evie spent that night with Michael but had to get up early the next morning to make it to Fort Hood on time. Although the two talked every day on the phone it was another two weeks before they went out again. This pleased Rubin who thought that they had, had an argument.

"Good morning Doctor Reilly." Rubin politely said as he walked into her office.

Not knowing what Rubin was doing she leaned back in her chair and gave him a big smile. "Good morning Rubin. When are you going to stop calling me Doctor. My name is Evelyn ... or Evie if you want."

"I'm sorry ... Evie." Rubin said. "I was just trying to keep it professional."

"But the only people around here that I do not call by name is the Colonel and two Lieutenants." she argued. "Some I call by their first name and some by their last name. I call you Rubin because I do not know your first name."

"It's John but most people around here just call me Rubin." he told her. "I don't really like the name John."

"Why not?" Evie asked.

"My father was abusive to my mother." Rubin said. "I am not a Junior but his first name was John too. Calling me John brings back to many bad memories."

"Oh wow! I understand now." Evie agreed with him. "Okay then I'll keep calling you Rubin."

"Thank you Evie." Rubin said and then left Evie's office as quickly as he came in. He left smiling thinking that he made a few points with her.

Evie felt bad for Rubin. The life he lived as a child must have been traumatizing. What Evie did not know was that

51

Rubin's story about his father being abusive to his mother was a lie. He was hoping to gain Evie's sympathy and in time her love. He had heard one time that women that felt sympathetic to a man often fell in love with them. He was going to play this lie out as well as he could.

The next day just by chance Rubin met Doctor Richards in the lunchroom. Richards told Rubin how he came up with the design of the tracking chips used in Michael Gibbins. When Richards mentioned Michael's name he got Rubin's attention.

Richards told Rubin many things about the chips and that they had found out that someone sent a feedback signal to Michael's chip that fried the chip. Then Richards told Rubin that the new chip had been removed and then placed just under the skin in Michael's right armpit. Rubin now knew why Michael had no pain when he turned the knob up to increase the feedback loop. Michael's chip was no longer in his brain. Tis also explained why Evie was looking under Michael's arm. The feedback must have still caused some pain which she was checking out.

That next Friday evening when Evie got off of work she headed straight to Michael's home. It was almost dark when she pulled up to his home. When Michael heard her car he opened the front door and stepped out on the porch. Odie ran outside before Michael closed the door. Odie and Dog were in a mad dash to see which one could make it to Evie first.

There was Dog; a large dog with long legs almost three times taller than Odie's head. And then there was Odie whose legs were no longer than about five to six inches. Odie's head was no taller than ten inches from the ground. However; Odie was the one that made it to Evie first but, when Dog got there she gave him a bunch of loving as well.

Evie had to push both dogs back just to get out of her car. She was finally able to get out of her car as she laughed all the way. Michael just stood on the porch not helping her at all. She was having a blast with the two dogs and he knew it. Finally she was on the porch giving Michael a big hug.

Once inside Evie went straight back to the main bathroom

where she took a shower. Then she came out wearing a very skimpy nightgown. "See anything you like?"

Michael gave her a quick look and then said; "Nope. Not really."

Evie stormed over to Michael and dropped herself in his lap. "Oh the nightgown." Michael said. "Was that what you were talking about?"

"You know it was." Evie said.

Michael started smiling and Evie did not like it. She quickly crossed her arms but still lay back against Michael. He wrapped his arms around her and they watched the TV.

The next day was Saturday. As usual Michael woke up around 3:00 a.m. and made a pot of coffee. After pouring himself a mug he went outside and sat in his chair on the porch. He and Evie had a big day planned. Evie wanted to go to the Mall but Michael saw that as a girly thing. He did not like the city. But as long as he was with her it didn't matter. When he went back in the house for his second mug of coffee he sat on the couch to watch his Fox News.

As he turned the TV on he heard movement in the kitchen. His moving around had waken Evie. After she got her a mug of the liquid ambition she sat beside Michael.

A couple of hours later Michael and Evie got dressed and left for the Mall. Michael lived far out in the country so it took almost an hour to get to the nearest Mall.

Being a Saturday the Mall parking lot was full. It took a good thirty minutes to find a parking spot for his truck. Once inside Evie went straight for the nearest clothing store. Michael kept a smile on his face as Evie went from one dress rack to another. Finally he told Evie to enjoy herself. He was going out to the walking area to sit down.

Michael watched Evie as she went crazy going through all of the dresses and pantsuits. Then she worked her way to the jewelry and perfumes. From time to time Michael lost sight of Evie but after a few seconds he would spot her. After about an hour she came walking out to Michael. During that entire time she bought nothing except for a tiny bottle of perfume that

Michael did not like. What looked like an hour of torture for Michael was really an hour of watching the woman of his dreams enjoying herself. He enjoyed seeing her happy.

As Michael and Evie started to move on to the next store five young punks rounded the corner and ran right into Evie knocking her down. Michael reached down and helped her up and then gave the taller punk a mean look. The five boys were part of a local gang called The Broods.

"Watch where you're going." the eighteen year old boy yelled at Evie.

"Are you always a punk or is it only when you try to be?" Michael asked.

The boy flipped out a knife and held it close to Michael's face. "Apologize or I'll cut you up."

Michael looked into the boy's eyes and started to slowly change. Then he quickly grabbed the knife from the boy's hand with one hand and the boy with the other hand. By time the boys knew what was happening they found themselves face to face with a six and a half foot tall mad Neanderthal. Michael slung the boy he had a hold of across the walkway; a good twenty feet. The other four pulled their knives but they could not get close to the beast. An invisible force was pushing them back and away from the beast. Suddenly the beast raised his arms and yelled so loud that people outside heard him. He looked at Evie and then turned and ran outside. Once outside he ran into the trees at the edge of the parking lot.

As the beast ran out of the Mall women and children were screaming. The five punks that started the whole thing left the Mall before security got there. Evie stood the for only a moment until she decided to leave. She did not want to have to answer any questions about the man that was with her. Once she was outside she looked around for Michael. After about an hour of looking around she went to Michael's truck. Not having a key so she could get into the truck she worried about how she was going to get home. Suddenly a hand sat down on her shoulder.

Evie whipped around to see that the hand belonged to

Michael. He had almost completely changed back to human form. He said nothing to her but handed his keys to her. She unlocked the passenger side door and helped him into the seat. After strapping the safety belt around him she closed his door. Then she went to the driver's side and got in.

It was still daylight when Evie drove into Michael's driveway. By then Michael was a little tired as the change took energy from him leaving him tired every time. Evie helped him into his home and into the bedroom where she allowed him to fall on the bed. She slung his feet onto the bed and took off his boots and socks. Then she went into the den and allowed him to sleep it off.

Back at Fort Hood Rubin was arguing with the Colonel about bringing Michael in and locking him up. "You've had to lock up all of the others in that underground ... cave in northern Oklahoma. Now he's out of control."

Maybe I should bring him in again." the Colonel said. "At least this time he didn't kill anyone."

Colonel Dillard sent Sergeant Bails and just two soldiers in his Limousine to get Michael. Bails was to ask Michael to come with him. No other soldiers would be sent this time except one driver and one sitting in the back with Bails and Michael.

Rubin was pleased with himself. With any luck Michael would be sent to the underground cells in Oklahoma for the rest of his life and then Evie might come to him.

Just under an hour after laying on the bed Michael walked into the den. He was scratching his eyes. Evie jumped up and gave him a big hug.

"How are you feeling Baby?" Evie asked Michael.

Michael only groaned as he continued to walk towards the couch. Evie helped him to walk as he was stumbling a little. As soon as he sat down Evie ran into the kitchen and got him a mug of coffee. She added the usual sweetener, milk, and chocolate syrup before filling the mug with coffee. A quick stir of a spoon dissolved the chocolate syrup and mixed everything together.

When Evie handed the mug of coffee to Michael he took a

sip and set it down on the end table beside him. "Thank you Babe." he said.

"Do you remember what happened?" Evie asked him.

Michael thought for a moment and then said; "Yeah! I do." Then he looked at Evie and asked; "Why hasn't the Colonel sent someone to get me?"

"Maybe he has and they just haven't got here yet." Evie said before realizing how depressing it sounded.

"Well I'll probably be locked up with the others this time." Michael quietly said.

Three hours later a black Limousine pulled into Michael's driveway. As Dog barked Sergeant Bails got out and patter him on the head. After giving Dog a little loving Bails walked up to Michael's front door. Michael opened the door before Bails even got to it and asked him to come in. He looked around and only saw the Limousine.

"Where are the two trucks of soldiers?" Michael asked the Sergeant.

"Colonel Dillard did not think there was any need for them." Bails replied. "That's how much he trusts you."

Michael looked at Evie and said; "Well if he was going to lock me up for the rest of my life he wouldn't just send his Limo."

"I'll fallow you back to the base." Evie insisted.

About three hours later the Colonel's Limousine pulled up to the front gate of Fort Hood. After the soldier realized who it was he flagged the Limousine through. Evie fallowed close behind it.

The soldier in the back seat with Michael was new at his job. When Michael got out of the car the soldier grabbed his upper arm as if he was going to escort Michael into the building. Michael stopped at looked at the soldier that still held on tight.

"Michael." Sergeant Bails said. "He's new. Try not to kill this one."

The soldier quickly let go of Michael's arm. Then he and Bails walked into the building smiling. They walked straight back to Colonel Dillard's office with Evie right beside Michael. Michael and Evie sat down in front of the Colonel's desk. A few minutes later the Colonel walked in and took his seat behind his desk.

Just as the Colonel started to speak Lieutenant Rubin walked into the office. "May I help you Lieutenant?" the Colonel asked Rubin.

Rubin was there on purpose but realized that if he caused any waves it might draw attention to what he was doing. "Oh! Sorry Sir." he said trying to look like he did not know that Michael was there. Then he turned his attention to Evie. "Hello Evie." he said with a smile that gave Evie goose bumps.

"Hello Rubin."

The Colonel interrupted and asked again; "May I help you Lieutenant?"

"I'll come back later Sir." Rubin quickly advised. "It was not important anyway." Then he quickly closed the door and went back to the Satellite Room. From there he tuned the satellite to watch the Colonel's meeting through the medal roof of the building. "To bad this satellite can't also listen in." Rubin whispered to himself.

"Well ..." the Colonel said. "At least this time you didn't kill anyone but you still changed in the eye of the public." Then he raised his voice. "In a Mall of all places. Are you crazy?"

"I don't think so Sir." Michael replied.

The Colonel calmed down. "Why did you do it?"

"He pulled a knife on me." Michael defended himself. "What was I suppose to do? Let him kill us both?"

"Of course not Michael but ..." the Colonel was not sure what he should have done. "If you cannot stop changing in public then maybe you should stop going out into the public."

Michael looked at Evie. "Now there's an idea. We can just stay at my home and ... just talk about it."

"Maybe in the bedroom?" Evie asked with a big smile.

"Hmmmm." Michael replied. "Now there's another idea."

"Okay you two." the Colonel said with his face cupped in his hands. "Come back to Earth now."

"Yes Sir." Evie whispered.

"What am I going to do with you Michael?"

"If you watched what happened you would have seen that he did control himself." Evie tried to help Michael.

"What control?" the Colonel asked. "He completely changed scaring the hell out of a Mall full of people and then ran off."

"What cover story did you use?" Michael asked.

"It will be in the local newspaper tomorrow how that an upcoming movie was being advertised but ... it did not go well."

"That sounds good." Michael said. He was not taking this seriously.

"I'm gon'a have to restrict you from going into the eye of the public Michael."

"How can you restrict me?" Michael asked.

"I can ask you to do it and then if you change in public again I'll have to take measures."

"What kind of measures?" Evie asked.

The Colonel looked sad. "If you change in public again I may have to confine you ... permanently."

"You would put me with the others?" Michael asked.

"Only if I had to. But I don't want to." the Colonel mentioned. "I need you to work with me Michael. Stay home or go fishing on your property. Just stay out of the eye of the public."

"I'll do that Sir." Michael promised. "I'll only go into town if I have to."

"Good enough." the Colonel said. "I need to let you know that if you do change in public I will be busted back down to Major and ... I would not be the one that locks you away." He took in a deep breath and then let it out. "They would."

"Who is They Colonel?"

"My superiors." the Colonel advised them.

Michael was released to go back home. As he and Evie walked to the door of the building they were stopped by Doctor Wheelhouse.

"I want to help you two out." Wheelhouse whispered. "The tracking chip is just under the skin of his right armpit."

But the Colonel didn't have the chip put back in him. Evie said.

"That's what he told you." Wheelhouse advised. "You can remove it Doctor Reilly but … he still needs to carry it with him or they'll bring him back in and put another chip in him."

"Why are you helping us?" Evie asked Wheelhouse.

"I don't know." Wheelhouse replied. "I just want to help. Take it out and run. Get away from the Colonel."

All of the way home Michael said very little to Evie. She could see that he was worried. When she drove into Michael's driveway Dog ran up to Michael's side of the car as he always did. Michael and Evie went into his home as quickly as they could.

Evie got some bacon from the refrigerator and cut it up in the crock pot. After adding some chopped onion and spices she boiled the bacon for about thirty minutes. Then she added the pinto beans. Michael loved his pinto beans and rice. In a few hours they would have a great meal.

As the beans cooked Evie looked at Michael's right armpit. She felt around and finally found a spot that was hard. That had to be the tracking chip. Using her fingernails she pulled the scab off causing some pain to Michael. Then she pulled out a tiny chip which she lay on a paper towel on the coffee table. With the chip out of Michael they could run but first they had to get away from the satellite that watched him all of the time.

Michael and Evie talked about what they should do as they watched a movie. It was a World War Two movie with Audie Murphy in it. The only thing on TV that was better than Audie Murphy was Fox News.

Chapter 6

The Final Straw

Two months went by and Michael did as he promised Colonel Dillard. He stayed on his property going into town only when he had to. Because of his having to stay away from the public he did more fishing than he had ever done. Every Friday evening Evie would come out and spend the weekend with Michael. At first she would go back to her own home on Sunday evening so that she could go to work the next day. But more and more often she started staying with Michael and left for work from there very early Monday morning.

During this time Evie worked with Michael trying to find out what exactly caused him to change. Evie did not believe that it was anger that did it. She believed that as he got angry he just did not care if he changed and then therefore changed into the beast. Michaels had learned to control his changing even better. The best things was that he could even change at will without even being angry. It was just a matter of getting out of the habit of changing just because he was mad about something.

Michael could change once or twice without being mad but he still had some problems. When Michael was the beast he still could not speak. He was still basically a wild beast just like the prehistory Neanderthal. He was also able to stop attacking the person or thing for which he changed. The beast had conscious thought of Michael but still remained a wild animal. In other words Michael knew what was going on when he was the beast but the beast was still wild. Michael could stop the beast from destroying something at will. He could now control the beast. There was one more thing about the beast.

When Michael changed into the beast Evie noticed that he could use a kind of force field. It was like a bubble that started around the beast and spread out away from him a few feet. Evie called this force field the shield. The shield would spread out away from the beast pushing tables, chairs, and even people in front of it. This had to have come from the alien DNA that he was given as a child.

Evie did not tell Colonel Dillard anything about this except that Michael was controlling the change even better. The Colonel was happy to hear this and asked Evie to bring Michael in sometime so that he could talk with him. When Evie talked with Michael about coming to see the Colonel he agreed.

Evie spent the fallowing weekend with Michael as she was starting to do every weekend. That Monday morning Michael came to Fort Hood with her. They met the Colonel in the lunchroom for breakfast. The Colonel knew that Michael liked his sausage, fried eggs and hash browns and made sure that there was plenty of it there for him.

Once Michael sat down with his plate full he started cutting the sausage, hash browns, and eggs up. Then he covered it with hot sauce and mixed it up. Evie and the Colonel watched Michael prepare his food and add the hot sauce. They were amazed as Michael began to eat the mixture. This was a side of Michael that Evie had only seen once.

Colonel Dillard started asking Michael questions but he and Evie had already talked about what to tell the Colonel and what not to tell him. Michael answered questions between mouth fulls of what was in his plate. Evie had to answer most of his questions for him. By time the three finished eating the Colonel had all of the answers that he needed.

"I'm proud of you Michael." the Colonel told him. "You have done what none of the others were able to do."

"It had a lot to do with Evie ... Doctor Reilly here." he admitted. "I could have done none of it without her help."

The Colonel shook Michael's and Evie's hands and went back to his office. He gave Evie the rest of the day off so she could take Michael home.

A few minutes after Michael and Evie left the Colonel went into the Satellite Room and talked with Lieutenant Rubin.

Rubin had been telling the Colonel what he was seeing when Michael and Evie were working on Michael's controlling his anger. However he was not exactly sure what he was seeing. He could tell that Michael was changing into the beast but he did not destroy anything. He just stood there as Evie talked with him. Unfortunately; that was all he knew.

What Rubin told the Colonel assured the Colonel that Michael and Evie had not told him everything. He considered that the same as lying. If they hid that information from him then what else were they hiding from him.

Rubin was trying to find something to get Michael in trouble with but the man was just to good. Then he looked at his monitor and saw something that shocked him. Seconds later Rubin ran into the Colonel's office.

"He's removed his tracking chip." Rubin told the Colonel.

The Colonel jumped up and fallowed Rubin back to the Satellite Room. The Colonel looked on as Rubin showed the satellite view of Michael and Evie driving down the highway. Then he showed the Colonel the tiny red flashing light showing where the tracking chip was. According to the tiny flashing light Michael was at his home but there he was traveling down the highway.

The Colonel stood straight and took in a deep breath. Letting it out he sent word for Sergeant Bails to meet him in his office. A few minutes later Bails stood in front of the Colonel's desk. The Colonel told the Sergeant what was going on and then ordered him to take two trucks to get Michael and bring him back. Doctor Reilly was to be arrested as well.

When Michael and Evie got back to his home they went inside. They were happy that the meeting with the Colonel went so well. Evie went into the kitchen to get them both a glass of ice tea. Michael started to sit down on the couch when he looked on the coffee table in front of him. There sat the zip lock bag with the tracking chip in it.

"Oh shit." Michael said to himself. Then he held up the bag and said; "Evie."

Evie looked at the bag in Michael's hand. She knew that it

was the bag with the tracking chip in it. "What about it?" she asked still smiling.

"I left it here … while we were at Fort Hood."

Evie stopped making the two glasses of tea and walked into the den. She took the plastic bag from Michael's hand and looked at it.

"I don't think the Colonel knows about this or he would not have allowed you to leave." Evie advised.

"He could have found out after we left." Michael wondered. "If he does know do you really think that he would send someone to get me?"

"Not someone but maybe a bunch of someones." she added.

"We talked about going on the run." Michael suggested. "You think that now would be a good time to do that?"

"No. Not yet anyway." Evie said. "I think no one caught it but you need to be more careful from now on."

What Michael and Evie did not know was that Sergeant Bails and two trucks of soldiers were almost at Michael's home. Michael and Evie sat on the couch and quietly watched the TV. They did not look like it but they were both in panic mode. Everything in them told them to run but Michael trusted Evie's feelings. About thirty minutes later there was a loud sound of big trucks pulling up.

Evie jumped up and ran to the front window. She saw about forty soldiers piling out of the two big trucks and surrounding Michael's home. By this time Michael was walking towards the door. Suddenly there was a knock at the front door.

Evie opened the door and saw Sergeant Bails standing there. Michael invited Bails inside but told the two soldiers behind him to stay outside. One of the soldiers tried to force his way in so Michael pushed him back.

"I'm fixing to kill you boy." Michael told the soldier.

Bails looked at the two soldiers and ordered them to stay outside. "Michael isn't gon'a to hurt me."

As the three sat down Evie asked bails what was going on.

Bails told them that the Colonel knew about the tracking chip. Then he saw the zip lock bag on the table and picked it up. Looking at the tiny chip in the bag he asked if that was what all of the fuss was about.

"I was sent to bring you both in." Bails said. "I even have a warrant for you Doctor Reilly."

"What for?" Evie asked. "You lied to the Colonel earlier." Bails said. "Actually the Colonel found out from Lieutenant Rubin that you did not tell him everything about Michael's progress.

"Lieutenant Rubin?" Evie asked.

"Yes Doctor." Bails said with his head down. "I don't know how far it goes but Rubin is not your friend. I think he is trying to get Michael into some kind of trouble."

"He did ask me out about a year ago but I turned him down." Evie advised.

"Oh! I bet that's it." Bails said. "No one tells Rubin no. Even the Colonel is scared to tell him he can not do or get something."

"Do you think he is stalking me maybe?"

"I don't know but he does seem to always know a lot about you both. It's like he is watching you two the entire time you're together." Then Bails stood and told Michael and Evie that they had to go.

"I don't think I'm going this time." Michael said.

"Oh I was hoping you wouldn't do this." Bails regrettably said. "There are forty well armed soldiers out there with orders to fire on you if you do not cooperate. Remember Michael that bullets can still stop the thing you turn into."

"The thing he turns into is called the beast." Evie said as she got angry.

"Michael." Bails said as he looked at the man. "I am your friend first and a soldier after that. But my hands are tied. I have no control over these soldier outside."

"I think that the best thing I can do is go with you." Michael said. "I don't want anyone hurt."

Bails let out a sigh of relief. He had not seen this beast that

Evie talked about but he had heard what happens when the beast came out.

Bails walked outside first so that the soldiers would not open fire on Michael. After him came Michael and then Evie. Michael started to get into the limousine but one of the soldiers stopped him and said that he was riding in the first truck. Michael continued to try to get into the limousine when the soldier hit him in the side of the head with the butt of his M-16.

Michael lay on the ground looking up at the soldier that was yelling at him. Michael was holding back and not changing. Evie thought that he was starting to change and yelled trying to stop him. Michael actually did stop changing but Evie was the only one that saw it. Suddenly the soldier used his rifle butt and pushed Evie back. Then he quickly hit her in the face with the butt of his rifle. That was it. No one hurts Evie.

Instantly Michael changed into the beast. Soldiers were flying all over the place. The beast looked down at Evie. She was out cold. The rage in the beast increased. A soldier fired a three round burst at the beast but the bullets ricocheted off of something covering the him before they even got to him.

"Stop." Sergeant Bails yelled.

All of the soldiers stopped what they were doing. The beast looked at Bails and then the soldiers.

"Stop Michael. They'll kill you." Evie said as she tried to get up.

The soldier that hit her with his rifle butt hit her again trying to shut her up. This time blood poured from her face as she lay on the ground motionless. The beast let out a blood curdling scream like he had never done before. Michael had never been this mad before. The shield around him widened pushing soldiers and even the limousine aside. Then the ground rumbled and a crack quickly formed opening up under twelve of the soldiers. After they fell into the Earth the crack closed killing all twelve. The beast started slapping soldiers as they fired their M-16 with no effect. When the beast stopped five soldier were left. They did not show any aggression against

Michael so he left them alone. The beast looked at Bails and lay his hand on his shoulder. Then he turned and ran into the woods to the east.

Back at Fort Hood Rubin and the Colonel was watching the carnage left by the beast. Twelve of the soldiers had vanished into the crack before it closed up on them and twenty three others lay badly wounded or dead. Only Sergeant Bails and five of the soldiers were left standing.

Colonel Dillard ordered five trucks and one hundred soldiers to Michael's home. He also order an Apache helicopter to get there as quickly as it could. If it found Michael or the beast then the pilot would order him to stand down. If he refused then the pilot was ordered to open fire and kill him.

Within thirty minutes the Apache was at Michael's home. As it circled the area the pilot told those on the ground through the PA speaker that more soldiers were on their way. Then it took off to look for the beast.

The beast kept to the thick trees and Yaupon bushes. After coming to the cool creak that ran into the lake the beast changed back to Michael. He was weak from such extreme anger. He had to find out more about Evie so he circled around to the northern side of his home. Michael walked closer to his home hoping to see if Evie wasp okay. Hiding about one hundred yards into the woods he crouched down so he would not be seen as he watched.

Evie was put in an ambulance and taken to a local hospital. As the soldiers walked around Sergeant Bails looked up and thought he saw someone but he was not sure. If it was anyone at all they were far back in the trees. He walked over to the edge of the woods and saw no one. If Michael was out there watching then he wanted to help.

As Bails walked farther into the woods he took a business card from his wallet and then returned his wallet back to his pants. Finally he saw someone trying to hide under a bush and walked over to the bush. Looking around as if he was really looking around he spoke.

"Is that you Michael?"

Michael hesitated to answer but still did. "Yes."

"Stay down and listen." Bails told Michael. He dropped the business card on the ground. "That is my card with my new cell phone number on it. That phone is not tapped. Call or text me if you need anything. Leave this area and forget about anything you have in your home. It will be watched now. When I walk out of here stay low and get out of here."

"What about Evie?" Michael whispered.

"She'll be okay." Bails said still looking around as if he was looking for someone. "I'll see to it myself but she might be arrested and punished for not telling the truth about you."

"Are you okay Sergeant?" one of the soldiers yelled from the edge of the woods.

"Yeah!" Bails yelled back. "Just looking around."

"That was close." Michael whispered.

"Yeah I know." Bails answered. "I need to get back to the others and you need to get out of here. Be careful for that Apache helicopter."

"I need some gear from my home." Michael said.

"Like I said … it will be watched." Bails reminded him. "I'll get a few things and put them in your backpack. No one will be watching me. I'll take that backpack with me and drop it in these trees in two days."

"Okay." Michael acknowledged. "See you in two days."

"Don't forget the card and call me when ever you need something." Bails reminded Michael as he turned and walked back to the others.

When Bails got back to the others he was asked what he was doing in the woods. He told the soldier that he had to relieve himself and he looked around while he was out there.

Michael was not sure what he could do. He had to hang around for two days waiting for Bails to go into his home and get a few things, put it all in his backpack and then drop it off in the woods. The woods behind Michael's home covered many square miles so that might hide him. A creek ran into the lake which gave him fresh water but he had no way to get any food.

Michael went to where the creek ran into the lake and set

up a small camp there. He had fished there many times. He built a crude lean-to for shelter and then walked around the bank of the lake. He found some old fishing string that he had cut off of his real because it was tangled up. As he worked on untangling the string he found an old rusty hook still attached to a short piece of string. By time he finished he had about nine feet of string with a rusty hook at one end.

After tying the string to a five foot long tree limb Michael looked around for any bait that he could use. After rolling over an old rotten log he found a few grubs. Placing one on the hook he tossed the line in the water where the creek flowed into the lake.

Within seconds Michael had caught a catfish. It was not a large one but it was something to eat. Before cleaning the catfish he started a fire so he could cook it. He feared that the smoke would give him away but he also had to eat. He even considered eating the catfish raw but decided against it. He cleaned the catfish and then stuck it on a green tree limb that he was able to break off. Now it was just a matter of time. It took a while but after a few turns of the fish it was finally cooked.

Michael got to thinking. The satellite must have lost him and without the tracking chip they could not find him. Otherwise he would have already been captured. Every once in a while he could hear the Apache helicopter flying off in the distance and put the fire out as soon as the fish was cooked. This was how Michael survived during the two very long days as he waited for Bails.

On the second day Michael stood to check on the backpack that Bails was suppose to drop off. As he turned he got the surprise of his life. Just ten feet in front of him were two Game Wardens.

"Are you Michael Gibbins?" one of the Wardens asked.

"No Sir." Michael said. "I'm Ray Gibbins. I have a cousin named Michael. This is his land."

"Do you have any ID on you?" the same Warden asked.

"No Sir. Why would I need my ID out here?"

"You're suppose to carry some sort of identification at all times."

"Sorry." Michael said with a kind smile. "Michael and I come out here every now and then to practice survival techniques. He must be running late."

"He will not be coming out here." the Warden said. "He's on the run from the law."

"Michael? What did he do?" Michael's acting would have won him an Oscar.

"He killed a bunch of people." the Warden advised.

"That's ... not Michael."

The Warden handing Michael his business card. "He is considered dangerous. Call me if you see him."

"Yes Sir." Michael continued to looked shocked. "By the way. Is he out here someplace? Is that why you're out here talking to me?"

"Smoke from your campfire was seen my a helicopter and reported to us. We came to check things out."

The two Game Wardens left but Michael knew that he could not hang around. He waited a while before going to check on his backpack. When he got close to the spot where he talked to Bails two days earlier he saw someone there. Instantly he hid and looked at the person. Finally he realized that the man was Sergeant Bails.

As Michael walked up Bails turned and smiled. "About time."

"I had two visitors looking for somebody named Michael Gibbins. I got rid of them but they may be back."

"Well here's your backpack." Bails handed the backpack to Michael.

"I need a phone or I cannot call you."

"I got you a new cell phone. It is in your backpack and don't worry about the monthly bills. I'll pay it for you." Bails told Michael. "You already had some things in the backpack ... fishing gear, two knives, and a two liter bladder. I just added a couple of changes of clothes and some of that survival food you had."

"Thanks a lot." Michael said as he gave Bails a hug. "What about Evie?" he asked.

"She's okay." Bails told him. "The charges against her have been dropped … by the Colonel. She'll be back to work in a few days. I'll let her know that you and I are in contact. She may want to join you."

"That wouldn't be good." Michael replied.

"I agree but you know Evie." Bails said with a big smile. "Evie does what Evie wants to do."

"Yeah I know." Michael said as he laughed.

"You just get out of here and try not to change into that beast. They'll know where you are if you do."

Michael turned and headed back into the woods. He worked his way out of the area. And off to the north. He had no idea where he was going but staying around there was out of the question. He had lost everything; a home, two great dogs, and a lot more. Now he was a wanted man and all because of something that his government did to him.

Michael wanted nothing more than to go back to Fort Hood and destroy that whole building; especially that Satellite Room. But could he still change at will? The night after he left Bails he sat by a campfire wondering that. He and Evie had only tried it a time or two. If he could change at will then he would do what he was wanting to do.

Michael concentrated. Without any anger he began to change. Although while he was the beast he had no control over some things likes speech he was still able to control what he as the beast did. He looked down at his massive hairy hands. He felt his face and the overhanging eyebrows. He was at that time the beast and he was in control of his actions. A minute later he was back to being Michael. He was able to change to the beast and back to human form at will.

That did it. He was going to give Fort Hood a visit.

Chapter 7

A Woman's Mind

After realizing that he could change into the beast and then back to human form at will Michael headed west towards Fort Hood. At times he took chances hitchhiking on the back roads but for the most part he walked. The only reason he did any hitchhiking was because he really did not expect to see anyone that knew him on the back roads. Sticking to walking through the woods took much longer but it was a lot safer.

It took four days to reach the back side of Fort Hood. He stood just inside the trees. The northern fence was still a good two hundred yards off. He knew that this was going to have to be a night job. However; as he looked beyond the fence he could not see the large medal building that had all of the offices and Satellite Room. He remembered seeing the fence just behind the building the last time he was there but something was wrong.

Michael went back deeper into the woods so that he would not be seen. There he waited until it got dark. As he waited he wondered if he could be at the wrong fence. He would have to check that out.

Michael knew that in order to get through the fence he would have to change into the beast. Also once he did break through the fence an alarm would probably go off. It was time to see just how fast the beast could run.

When it was dark enough to leave the cover of the trees Michael stepped closer to the edge of the woods. After changing the beast stepped out and tried to rip the fence open. It could not do it so it grabbed the bottom of the fence and pulled up making a large hold to crawl through. Then the beast looked around. Far off in the distance he could see another fence lined with lights with a large medal building on the other side. He ran as fast as he could.

Michael was surprised at how fast the beast could run and when he got to the other fence the beast was not even tired. He looked at the building and it was the one that held the Satellite Room. He pulled that fence up like he did the other one and went to the back door of the building. The question ran through his mind. *Should I hurt or kill anyone inside? No! I will only harm them if I had to.*

The beast made a fist and punched a hole in the back door. Then he ripped the door off of it's hinges. Finally an alarm went off.

The beast went straight to the Satellite Room and knocked down the door. There was no time to be human. A woman that Michael did not know was sitting at the Satellite screen. She stood and screamed. The beast gently pushed the woman aside and then started smashing everything in the room. By time the beast finished with the room armed soldiers were there.

One of the soldiers fired a round at the beast and to Michael's surprise it hit him in the side. Blood flowed from the side of the beast who instantly redefined the word anger. The beast gave that blood curdling yell that half of the people in Fort Hood could hear. Then he grabbed the soldier's M-16 and bent the barrel. The other two soldiers fired but their bullets ricocheted off of an invisible shield that surrounded the beast. *Maybe I only have the shield when I'm mad.*

The beast pushed the soldiers out of his way and continued his destruction of the offices and other rooms. But when he came to the lunchroom he left it alone. He destroyed all of the offices except for the office of Doctor Evelyn Reilly. By time the beast was ready to leave over three thousand rounds had been fired at the him with only the first one hurting him. Each time his side hurt his anger grew to the point that Michael was having a hard time controlling the beast. He knew that if he did not control the beast then it might destroy the entire base. It was time to leave before he did loose control.

With bullets flying all over the place the beast ran to the back door. After a quick look he ran past the two fences and into the woods. Three Apache helicopters fallowed the beast into the woods. The beast could not get away from them as they fired their fully automatic 30 millimeter cannons. The rounds exploded where ever they hit. The beast was fast but he could not out run the helicopters.

The beast stopped and turned. One of the 30 mm rounds hit the shield right at the face of the beast. His anger only increased. Looking around he found a few rocks and picked three of them up. When one of the helicopters came within sight the beast threw one of the rocks. The rock went through the windshield killing the gunner and caused the helicopter to crash. The crash killed the pilot.

When the second helicopter flew close to help the crashed one the beast threw another rock sending it to the ground as well. The third helicopter turned to get out of the area but the beast threw the third rock clipping it's tail. It also crashed but it was more of a controlled crash. The pilot and gunner survived.

The beast looked at the hold in his side. The bullet had gone in and exited a few inches away. It did not look all that bad but it hurt a great deal. The bleeding had stopped but he knew that when he changed back to human form it would heal.

With it being dark the beast began to run off to the north. Using the strength and speed of the beast Michael decided to remain as the beast for a while. When he felt that he was no longer being fallowed the beast changed back into human form. Far off in the distance he could hear small explosions; probably the 30 mm rounds from other Apache helicopters. For some reason they were thinking that he was still in that area. This meant that no satellite was watching him.

Michael looked at his side. The entrance and exit wounds were healed. He would have the scars to remember his ordeal. The pain was still there but it also would stop in time.

Two days later Michael was still hiding in the woods when his cell phone rang. It was Sergeant Bails.

"Well howdy." Michael said.

"I bet you're proud of yourself aren't you?" Bails asked

with a soft giggle in his voice.

"Actually I am." Michael advised. "What's the news?"

"Fort Hood released an article to the newspapers that they were training that night and that was the reasoning behind the explosions and all of the Apache helicopters." Bails replied.

"I expected that." Michael said as he laughed.

"Your picture is all over the news as a mass murderer." Bails said. "I would stay away from any public at all."

"I have to get food and other things from time to time."

"Just be careful Michael." Bails advised him. "There's a fifty thousand dollar reward for you."

"Wow! Does that make me important?"

"Important enough that anyone might turn you in."

"How is Evie?"

"She is returning to work tomorrow but don't call her. Her phone is tapped." Bails told Michael. "I did tell her that you and I were in contact with each other. I will call you in a few days when she will be with me so you two can talk."

Thanks man." Michael sighed heavily. "I really miss her."

"Got'a go Michael. You stay hidden and away from anyone."

"Warn Evie that I have grown a beard and mustache. I don't even look the same."

"Good idea but someone might still think they know you and have the police check you out. If the police run your finger prints you'll be caught."

"Yeah ... I know."

The two men said their good-bys and then hung up their phones. Michael continued to head north. It did not matter which direction he went as long as he stayed hidden.

A few days later Michael found himself in a homeless camp just south of Dallas. It was a large camp set up by a minister to help the homeless and was located on the church property. With the camp being on church property the city could do nothing about it.

As Michael made a few friends he told a story about how he lost his job and could not find another one. Then he lost everything including his home. He was quickly excepted by the others.

The truth was that he had plenty of money in the bank but surely the government confiscated it. Even if they had not he could not try to get any of it out. The transaction would be noted and the Colonel would know where he was.

Late one evening Michael was sitting on the back pew in the church when his phone rang. It was Bails.

"I have someone here that wants to talk to you." Bails told Michael. "But we don't know if my phone is tapped so you have two minutes."

"Baby?" Evie asked.

"Oh God it is so good to hear your voice." Michael said.

"Just listen." Evie insisted. "I need to find you. I want to be with you."

"No! Michael insisted. "If you are with me your life will be in danger."

"I don't care Michael. I love you and I want to be with you."

"Well I'm not telling you where I am." Michael replied. "I don't know where I am anyway. I do need one thing. Check and see if my checking account is being watched or if it's closed. I need money."

"Of course I will Baby but I want to be with you."

"Babe ... you can help me a lot more if you're out there doing things for me like checking my bank account."

Bails showed Evie his watch. "Fifteen seconds."

"I need to go Baby." Evie told Michael. "I love you and I'll call when I can."

"I love you too Babe." Michael said. Then there was a click and he knew that she or Bails hung up.

Michael stood and turned to find the minister standing behind him. "You were listening to my phone call?" he asked the minister.

"Yes I was ... Michael."

"You gon'a turn me in?"

"Nope." the minister assured him. "By the way. People

75

around here call me Brother Mason."

"Why aren't you going to turn me in?" Michael wanted to know. "I think the reward is fifty thousand dollars."

"I know but ... then I would have to answer to God for doing it."

"But turning in someone for a lot of money that can help your church is not a sin." Michael said.

"It is when you promise God not to do any harm." Brother Mason replied.

"You want to know what happened? Michael asked.

"I know what the government is saying happened but I am sure that you have another story."

Brother Mason sat down beside Michael as he told the minister what happened. Mason was amazed that the story about a Neanderthal running around was actually true. Then Mason got up. It was time to serve the evening meal that he always did. He and Michael had a bond now so Michael helped in carrying the pots of stew out to the table in the middle of the camp. Then he helped in serving the others there.

Mason stood back and looked at Michael helping out. He instantly saw that Michael was a good man. What the government had done to him did not change that. It just made him change into a monster with a good heart. The sudden urge to help Michael flowed through Mason's body. He took that as God telling him to help Michael. That was when he decided to help Michael in any way he could.

Evie was excited about talking to Michael. She wanted so much to be with him but if she left her job the Colonel would know that she was with Michael. It would be easier to find two people than just one. Michael grew a beard to cover his face but she could do nothing. Then again!

When Evie got off of work she headed straight for the Mall. She called Bails and begged him to meet her there. He had no wife or girlfriend to report to so he agreed.

About an hour later Bails walked in the main doors of the Mall. On both sides of the entrance area were a line of benches.

Far to his left he saw Evie sitting there reading her Kindle. When she looked up and saw Bails walking up to her she jumped up almost dropping her Kindle.

"I have a great idea and I want to see what you think." Evie said with a big smile.

"Okay then." Bails replied as he was pulled by the hand into the section of the Mall where the stores were. Letting go of Bails' hand she quickly walked; almost ran into a wig shop. After trying on different wigs for about thirty minutes she decided on a red wig.

"Well how does it look?" she asked Bails.

"Is this all you wanted?" an aggravated Bails said through his teeth.

"I'm trying to look like someone else so I can go be with Michael." Evie confessed.

"Woe, woe there Princess." Bails stopped her. "If you do that you will get both of you caught or killed."

Evie did not listen to anything Bails said. Her mind was on seeing her man again; at any cost. Once Evie paid for the long red wig she left the store and went down a ways to a Western Wear clothing store. Evie always wore a dress so no one ever saw her wearing blue jeans and a button-up shirt.

After buying two pair of blue jeans and two button-up shirts they left the store and went to a shoe store. She tried on many western boots but did not like them to much. Finally she found a pair that felt good so she bought them.

"Now can you fallow me back to my place?" Evie asked Bails. It was a question that he had always wanted to hear a woman ask him but he knew that Evie had no interest in him.

The two got in their cars and drove back to Evie's apartment. Once inside Bails sat on the couch and turned on the TV. Fox News was talking about how the Democrats were nothing but Communist and how they both acted the same. Evie went into her bedroom. A few minutes later Evie walked out of her bedroom for Bails to see.

"Well what do you think?" Evie asked Bails.

"Wow!" he said unable to say anything else. "Maybe you

can pull this off after all. You don't even look close to the same."

"I always wear make-up unless I'm with Michael." Evie said. "He doesn't like it. So no one has seen me without my make-up. How do I look?"

"Like I said. You don't even look close to the same." Bails said. "But we still don't know where Michael is."

Evie looked down. All of that work to change her appearance was for nothing. "I'll just set this all aside until we find where he is." she told Bails.

Evie was depressed. She wanted nothing more than to be with her man. Most of the offices in the building had been repaired so Evie was able to go back to work in her office. She had been sharing a desk with two other people. Now she was back in her office. The beast had not hurt her office but part of the building caved in ripping the roof above her office. That roof had to be fixed before she went back to her office. Evie sat at her desk. With her elbows on her desk and he face in her hands she prayed.

"Father ... please help me. I want so much to be with Michael. He needs me. Please Father. Show me where he is. Please protect him and keep him safe. I leave him in your hands now Lord. You know how I feel but ... let your will be done ... not mine."

Two days later a Private came into her office and advised her that she had a visitor at the gate; a Brother Mason. Brother Mason said that it was important. She did not know any Brother Mason but was wanting to see who it was anyway. She told the Private to please escort the man to her office. Thirty minutes later the Private and two well armed soldiers escorted an old man dressed in black into Evie's office.

"I'm Pastor Mason." the old man said.

"I'm sorry Sir but I don't know you."

"Oh yes you do." Mason said with a big smile. "You and Michael dropped by my church one time."

"He and I are Christians but I don't remember seeing you before today." Evie insisted.

Mason quickly leaned forward and whispered; "I have word from Michael."

It took a few seconds for what Mason had said to sink into Evie's head but it finally did. "Oh Pastor Mason. Of course."

Pretending to remember him Evie ran around her desk and gave Mason a big hug. Then she turned her attention to the soldiers. "He's a distant cousin from Ireland. I'll escort him back to the gate when he leaves."

"Yes Ma'am." One of the soldiers said as he closed her door behind them.

"I am Irish but how did you know?" Mason asked.

I didn't." Evie quickly admitted. "Now how is Michael?"

"He's just fine working at my church." Mason told her. "And yes I know who he is and what he changes into. I'm his friend so you do not have to worry about me."

Evie quickly gave Mason another big hug. The two talked for a while and then she decided to take off work early. She called Bails on the intercom and asked him to come to her office. When he opened the door to Evie's office he quickly stopped. He did not know who the old man was and was startled to see him standing there.

"This is an old friend ... Pastor Mason." Evie said as she waved her hands for him to close the door. Once the door was closed she whispered to Bails that Mason had news from Michael.

"What do you two say that we go out and get something to eat." Bails said loud enough for anyone in the hall to hear. Then he whispered; "We can talk there."

Mason and Evie agreed. As they walked to their cars Colonel Dillard walked up to Evie.

"Taking off early?" the Colonel asked.

"Yes Sir. This is a distant cousin from Ireland." Mason and the Colonel shook hands and then the Colonel left for his office.

Evie, Bails, and Mason got in their cars and drove to a Chinese restaurant with a large buffet.

Once they were in the restaurant Evie insisted on paying for all three meals. They got their food and sat at their table. Before talking Evie insisted on praying over the meal.

"Thank you Father for bringing us together today." Evie started crying but quickly stopped. *"Help us to get done what needs to be done. I miss Michael Father. We thank you for this food that you have given us. Please bless it and make it nourishment to our bodies. Amen."*

Mason started talking first. "Michael walked into my homeless camp one day but I knew his story was not that of a homeless man. Then I saw the picture of this wanted man on the TV that night. The next day I walked into the church and he is talking to a woman ... I think you Evie. She must have said that she loved him because he said he loved her too."

"That was me." Evie mentioned. "But please go on."

Mason took in a deep breath and let it out. "Well ... he told me who he was but I already knew. I assured him that I was not going to turn him in. He's helping me out a lot at the church now."

Why did you not turn him in?" Evie asked. "He's worth fifty thousand dollars you know."

"Well Evie ... it's like this." Mason said with a big smile. "God told me to help the man out so I am doing that."

Evie started crying again. "It's okay Evie." Mason said. After we eat I'll be taking you to him."

After the three ate they all went to Evie's apartment. She packed her backpack and then changed into her new clothes; her new look. As she continued to get things ready Mason and Bails sat down.

"By the way Evie." Mason said. "You'll be leaving your car here."

"I'll be doing what?" Evie loved her car. "I'm still making payments on it."

"You're not making payments on anything anymore." Mason mentioned. "It's your car or Michael. Make up your mind."

"Well of course it's Michael." She said.

"When you fail to come to work tomorrow they will start looking for your car." Mason advised her. "Then when they find it they will find you … and Michael.

"He's right Evie." Bails said. "If you want to be with Michael then you will have to give up any life you have right now."

"Okay then." Evie agreed. "I can do this."

"As long as you're with Michael I think you can do anything." Mason said.

Bails helped Evie to pack her things in Mason's car. She also added a large walk-in tent because Mason had said that Michael did not have one. He was sleeping inside the church itself like some of the others without tents did.

Before climbing into Mason's car Evie turned and gave Bails a hug. "You've been a great friend. Thanks for all that you have done for Michael."

"He has a cell phone." Bails suggested. "Leave your phone here in your car. They can track you through the GPS on your phone. Only use his phone when calling me."

Evie tossed her phone into her car and locked the doors. Then she climbed into Mason's car. Bails stood there and watched Mason's car disappear off in the distance. He had two good friends out there on the run from the federal government. He had done all he could to help them. Now it was up to Brother Mason.

Chapter 8

Sanctuary

Mason and Evie pulled into the church parking lot about three hours after leaving Evie's apartment. She had left her entire life behind. She had made the decision to walk away from the life she knew and start running with Michael. She left a high paying job, security, an apartment, and new car to start living in poverty but, it was worth it. Michael was worth it.

"There he is Evie." Mason told her. "Walk up close to him and see if he recognizes you."

Evie got out of Mason's car and looked at the love of her life. Dressed up in western boots, blue jeans, a short sleeve button-up shirt and a straw cowboy hat Evie walked out to Michael. For a few minutes she stood close to Michael with him looking at her a few times but not realizing who she was. Then Mason walked up.

"Ha Brother Mason." Michael said. "You got back from Houston pretty quick."

"I didn't go to Houston Michael." Mason assured him. "I went someplace else."

"Well it's good to have you back."

"Tell me something Michael." Mason mentioned. "What would it be worth to you to see … what's her name… oh yes … Evie?"

"Oh God I miss her but you know my story." Michael said as he looked down. "I cannot have her out here with me … living like this."

"And what if she wanted to be with you no matter what it cost her?" the woman beside Michael said.

That voice. Michael thought to himself. "Evie?"

Instantly the two hugged each other for a long time. Then Michael remembered the dangers of Evie being with him.

"What are you doing?" Michael snapped at her. "Being with me you will be arrested with me or killed with me."

"I don't care anymore Baby." Evie said. "I gave up my entire life just to be with you. I love you Michael and your life is my life." As Michael hugged Evie again he looked at Mason.

"She did Michael." Mason told him. "She gave up everything and now she could not go back even if she wanted to … and I don't think she wants to."

Evie walked Michael over to Mason's car and got her things out of the car. Then they set up the tent. Evie also brought two sleeping bags which they opened up all the way. Placing one on top of the other they made an almost soft bed. They would cover up with blankets from the church.

Once their tent and bed was set up there was nothing that they wanted more than to zip up the door to the tent and; talk. The more they looked around the more that issue pressed on their hearts and minds. Finally they gave into their animal instincts and zipped up the front door flap for privacy. Then they; talked.

Michael and Evie thought that they had fooled everyone there but they had fooled no one. As Mason talked to the others they started asking him who this new woman was. He only told them that she was Michael's girlfriend and they had not seen each other for a long time. He told them that the two were very much in love. Everyone there liked Michael very much; quite an achievement for someone that had only been there a few days. After hearing what Mason had to say about Michael and Evie they understood the two having a desire to be alone; so they could talk.

After about an hour the front of the large tent opened and Michael stepped out. Those around their tent cheered as if Michael had done something great. It was more of a joke. Evie stepped out to see what was going on and she also got a cheer from everyone there.

"Come meet everyone." Michael told Evie. "They're great people."

Holding her hand Michael took Evie around to meet some

of the people. As they talked with Evie she learned that their main fear was the city closing down the camp which was named Sanctuary. The city wanted to shut down the place but it was on church property. The people there kept the camp clean giving the city nothing to shut them down for. There was that one campfire that the city tried to use but the church took the city to court and won. They were allowed to have one campfire which served as light at night and a central area for everyone to sit and talk during the day and night.

That night Michael and Evie sat around the campfire and talked with the others. They continued to talk about the city's desire to shut Sanctuary down. If the city was to win then none of these people knew where they would go. The Mayor was a Socialist and even ran on that. That meant that the people elected a man that was basically a Communist. It was hard to believe that, that would happen in the United States.

Suddenly Sanctuary had over one hundred police officers standing at the main gate to the church property. The homeless people there were scared. Mason walked out to the gate and a piece of paper was passed through the gate to him. As he held a flashlight to read the paper he got mad and threw the paper on the ground. Then he said something to the man that passed the note to him and then turned. When he got back to the campfire he told everyone that in one hour the police were coming in and evicting everyone.

Michael tried to think about what he could do. If he changed to help everyone out then Colonel Dillard would know that he was there or at least in that area. Then he saw the motor vehicles behind the police and got an idea. Asking Evie to stay there he got up and walked to the fence at the back of the property.

Just before changing he saw Evie standing there. "Watch but stay here. I'll be backing a few days."

Slowly Michael changed into the beast. Not wanting to hurt church property the beast lifter the fence just enough to crawl under it. Then he walked around to the vehicles behind the police. There he saw one armored ramming vehicle. It looked like a tank with a ramming pole where the gun usually was. There were also two military type Humvees. A large van with the words SWAT Team on the side of it.

The beast looked over the ramming vehicle and then grabbed the ramming arm. After bending it a man crawled out of the top. Seeing the beast he jumped down. The beast turned the ramming vehicle over on it's top and left it like that. Then he went to the SWAT van and looked at the police officer in driver's seat. When the driver saw the beast he started shaking. The beast gave the officer a growl and the driver passed out from fear. Then the beast picked up the front of the van and shook it hoping to make anyone in the back run out. It worked. When the last officer ran out of the van the beast started smashing it. This made a lot of noise causing the police officers at the gate to run back to the vehicles. As the beast continued to smash the SWAT van some of the officers opened fire on him. Two of the bullets hit the beast before he could put up his shield. With the van smashed and with two new bullet holes in him the beast turned his attention to the police officers. Now full of anger he had his shield up.

The beast rushed at the officers but he had no intentions on harming anyone. As the police officers ran from the charging beast he turned and ran the other way. It took a while but he found his way into the dark where he changed back to human form. Then he spent the next day heading north. He had to draw any attention to a spot north of Sanctuary to make it look like the beast was just coming through that area.

A few days later Michael walked into a fast food store. Looking around he saw only two cameras. He still had a few dollars and bought a few things including a razor to shave with. Then he went back to a bridge that crossed over a creak. Once there he saved his beard and mustache off. When he did something to draw attention to the beast he wanted to change back to human form in front of all there. He wanted them to see him with out a beard and tell the police what he looked like. He wanted the Colonel to know that it was him.

Michael spent the rest of the day under the bridge. He

stuffed the few things he had far up under the bridge so no one coming by would take it. Then just as it was starting to get dark he went back out and to a different store. Standing between two buildings Michael changed into the beast. Then he rushed into the store trying to look confused. Two women passed out. He walked over to a man standing close to him and placed his hand on the man's shoulder. Then he changed back to human form for all to see.

"Sorry folks." he said as a human. Then he turned and ran out.

Michael ran back to the bridge and found that some kids were going through his things. When they saw him they dropped Michael's things and ran. Michael got the few things he had and left the area heading back to Sanctuary.

By time Michael found his way back to Sanctuary he only had a few days growth of a beard. It was not enough to hide who he was so Mason allowed him to sleep in the church basement a few days. No one in Sanctuary except Mason and Evie knew that he was there.

Mason credited the beast with stopping the police from evicting everyone in Sanctuary. He told Michael that when the police lost their vehicles and saw that their bullets had no affect on the beast they gave up what the mayor wanted them to do. Come to find out the eviction was illegal anyway. An attorney that was sympathetic to the homeless took their case and filed a law suit against the city and especially the mayor. The judge ordered the mayor to stop all actions against the homeless camp named Sanctuary.

Michael also found out that the day after the beast destroyed the police vehicles Colonel Dillard and at least one company of soldiers came into the camp asking questions. It was funny but not one person living in Sanctuary saw a thing. The police had many other stories though.

Sergeant Bails was also there. First he saw Pastor Mason and pretended not to know him. When he was alone with Mason he asked where Michael and Evie were. Mason told Bails that Evie ran into the church and was hiding in the basement. Michael, on the other hand, ran off after the beast destroyed the police vehicles. Colonel Dillard and his soldiers stayed in the area until they heard that the beast had been seen in southern Dallas.

For a while the Colonel chased false reports of the beast being seen all over north Texas and into Oklahoma. The farther the Colonel was from Sanctuary the better everyone in Sanctuary felt.

After three weeks Michael's beard was long enough that he could come out of the basement. He did this at night so that no one would see him coming out of the church basement. Evie even had to act surprised to see him as if he just came back.

One day Michael and Evie walked into town to try to find a job as many of the homeless did. Mainly Michael was the one that looked for a construction job. Other than being clean of any drugs most companies did not care about a man's life. Many that worked construction had been in prison at least once. A few of them had spotless records or no criminal records at all.

Those that lived at Sanctuary got a raw deal from almost everyone in the area. Most of the people in the area considered them to be the lowest of trash; bums that had no desire to improve their lives. Store owners would not hire them. Although they were clean some of the local people even held their noses as they walked by someone from Sanctuary.

The truth was that those living at Sanctuary were hard workers that just had bad luck. The church had set up four showers; two for the men and two for the women and small children. By around four in the evening Michael and Evie came back to Sanctuary. They took their showers and then waited to eat the evening meal.

The church women that cooked the evening meals for those living there were running late. They usually served the evening meal around 5:00 p.m. but it would be served around 6:00 p.m. that day. This was perfect as Michael and Evie were late getting back.

Sitting around the campfire that night many of those there

complained about no one wanting to hire them. In many cases a less qualified person was hired over a highly qualified person that lived at Sanctuary.

A few days later while Evie was taking a shower another woman walked up to Michael. She was just over five feet tall and very beautiful. Having no man to help take care of her she was interested in Michael.

"You're Michael?" she asked.

"Yes." Michael cheerfully answered her. "May I help you?"

"My name is Brady; Brady Willis." she said as she stuck out her hand to shake his.

Brady held on to Michaels hand until he actually had to pull his hand from hers. "I saw you the other night."

"I've been here a while so you probably have." Michael said with a smile.

"I saw you and your wife walking around in the moonlight." she said.

"Evie and I love each other but we are not married."

"Oh!" Brady replied. "That's good." she said before thinking about it. "I mean ... I'm sorry. I don't know what I meant."

Michael was laughing. "That's okay. I get that a lot."

Brady looked up and saw Evie walking back so she told Michael that she would see him later. Then left.

"Who was that?" Evie asked Michael.

"Just someone living here." Michael told her. "But there's something stange about her."

"Strange in what way?"

"I don't know." he said as he watched Brady walk away.

"Well ... I'm clean if you want to look at me." Evie suggested.

Michael looked at Evie with a big smile. "Getting jealous?"

"Should I be?" Evie said while pretending to be upset.

Michael and Evie went into their tent. Michael zipped up the front flap so they could have some privacy to; talk. About an hour later they came out to help with the evening meal. It was something that they started doing every day.

It was a requirement for those living there that they go to church on Sunday morning. They did not have to go to Pastor Mason's church as long as they went to a church. Mason's church that helped the homeless was a Baptist church. Michael and Evie were mostly non-Denominational Christians but they enjoyed Mason's preaching. He was well educated in the Bible.

Colonel Dillard was still fallowing false leads. Stories of the six and a half foot tall Neanderthal spread across the country but more and more stories had him saving lives. Before long the public had a love of the creature. In many cases the stories told of this Neanderthal being a hero.

One story from Beaumont, Texas told of a tall, hairy stranger that saved the lives of three boys that had been kidnapped by a crazy man. The man had the boys tied up in a home where he had the police held back. The police did not want to attack the home out of fear that they might harm the boys. Of course tear gas was out of the question. The man held the police back for two days when suddenly a tall hairy beast crashed through the back door and killed the man.

The three boys said that a caveman broke through the back door and grabbed the man and threw him through the front window of the home. Then the; caveman as the boys described him; untied them and took them to the front door. No one but the three boys saw the tall, hairy creature that the boys described.

Another story came from a small Oklahoma town just north of the Texas border. In this story a small mom-and-pop store was being robbed by four gang members of a local gang. Suddenly something that looked just like a prehistoric Neanderthal opened the front door and came in, grabbed the gang members one by one and threw them out through the all glass door. One of them died of massive cuts and the other three did not argue when the police got there. Only the store owner and the four gang members saw the Neanderthal.

Some of the stories were so ridiculous that the Colonel refused to even check the story out. Of course these stories were made up by those there. The whole time Michael and Evie were at Sanctuary.

Not finding anything creditable Colonel Dillard went back to Fort Hood. He had been gone for almost two months with the only creditable story coming from the homeless camp south of Dallas called Sanctuary. Over one hundred police and other citizens there told stories of a large caveman looking creature smashing the police vehicles. The police were there to evict the homeless from Sanctuary. *Was Michael trying to protect his new home?* the Colonel wondered.

Not knowing that Sergeant Bails was talking to Michael and Evie every now and then he called the Sergeant in his office. A few minutes later Bails walked into the Colonel's office and stood at attention.

"At ease Sergeant." he said. "Take a seat."

Bails sat down in the chair in front of the Colonel's desk hoping that he had not been found out. He started breathing easier when the Colonel told him about his suspicion that Michael and Evie might be in Sanctuary. He ordered Bails to find a man that could infiltrate the homeless at Sanctuary. He needed to pick a man that Michael and Evie did not know. If this man spotted either Michael or Evie he was to do nothing but report back to Bails who would report to the Colonel.

That night Bails called Michael and told him what the Colonel was doing. Once he picked the man he would text Michael with the man's picture. However; Michael thought that it might be best if he and Evie left Sanctuary until the man had gone back. Bails agreed.

The next day Bails talked to a few men for the job but the Colonel decided to use someone from Army Intelligence. After all. They were trained for doing this. The problem was that the Colonel did not tell Bails what he did.

That evening Bails brought a soldier to see the Colonel. The Colonel did not talk to the soldier much but at least learned his name. He was Corporal Sam Riggis. The Colonel explained his mission and then the Corporal left. He was taken to within two blocks of Sanctuary and got out of the car to walk the rest of the way.

Army Intelligence sent a Lieutenant Randy Piles to the Colonel's office. After telling the Lieutenant his mission he was also taken to within two blocks of Sanctuary and let out of the car to walk the rest of the way. The Lieutenant knew about the Corporal that Bails sent but neither the Corporal nor Bails knew about the Lieutenant.

That evening Bails took off early and called Michael. He told him about the Corporal who may or may not use his real name. After talking to him he text Michael with a picture of the Corporal.

Lieutenant Piles took a few hours longer to get to Sanctuary. He was a smart man trained to do just this; infiltrate a group and do what was needed to be done. Like the Corporal he was only to report back but directly to the Colonel; not Bails.

Mason knew that it would be best for Michael and Evie to get out of Sanctuary. He called a good friend who was a Catholic Priest. Father Williams agreed to hide Michael and Evie for as long as it was needed. His church also had a homeless camp that Dallas was trying to shut down. Mason drove Michael and Evie to the Catholic church homeless camp. It was named Camp Mc Farlin after the first Irish priest at the church. He was the one that started the homeless camp. Just fifteen minutes after Mason drove out of Sanctuary Corporal Sam Riggis walked into Sanctuary. He had no tent and was allowed to sleep in the church.

About two hours later Lieutenant Randy Piles walked into Sanctuary. He also had no tent and was allowed to sleep in the church. As Piles walked into the church he instantly spotted the Corporal. On the other hand Sam did not know Randy from anyone else there.

Mason got back to Sanctuary just after it got dark. He had seen the picture of the Corporal and knew Sam as soon as he saw him. He was introduced to Sam and Randy. He asked if they had eaten and both said no so the worker took them to the kitchen where the stew was warmed up for them. Sam and

Randy ended up being good workers helping Mason when ever needed.

Chapter 9

Maria

Michael and Evie settled into their new home at Camp McFarlin. They had left their tent back at Sanctuary but Father Williams allowed them to sleep in the church basement. He gave them two sleeping bags. They helped Father Williams with anything he needed but mostly with the two meals that the church gave the homeless that lived there.

Not just any homeless person could not get into Camp McFarlin. Like in Sanctuary anyone living in Camp McFarlin had to actively look for work or except work offered to them. This included doing things for Father Williams or his church. It was also required that everyone living there go to church; any church.

Camp McFarlin was a little more strict on cleanliness than Sanctuary was. Every Saturday was Clean Camp Day. The place was already clean but the showers and restrooms, kitchen and all pots and pans were cleaned. The pots and pans were cleaned as soon as the food was out of them but the kitchen could always use a little more attention. These were things used by the homeless there and became the responsibility of the homeless living there. Anyone that refused to help was asked to leave. If they refused to leave then there were always a few men that would help them leave. Anyone kicked out was not allowed to return.

On Sunday mornings Michael and Evie took their showers and then walked one block down the road to an Assembly of God Church. That was the closest they could get to Non-Denominational. The pastor there was a young man named Brother Mike Gilmore. Knowing that Michael and Evie were not Catholic Father Williams did not care that they did most of their work for Brother Gilmore. In the Father's words; "At least they are working for God."

It did not matter where Michael and Evie went they were liked. People in both the Catholic and Assembly of God churches thought highly of them. Finally one day
a woman in the Assembly of God Church offered a job for both of them.

Maria Sanchez was eighty-eight years old and had plenty of money to hire them both. Michael would take care of everything outside and Evie took care of Maria and the inside of her home. She also was responsibility for all meals. They even had their own bedroom with a bathroom.

Maria only paid them minimum wages but she took care of all of their needs. They ate their meals with Maria and they even watched TV together at the end of the day. Before long the three were getting along real good. They were like a small family.

Late one evening Michael got another phone call from Bails.

"How are you two doing?" Bails asked.

"Real good now." Michael said. "We're working for a woman at her home. I take care of things outside and Evie takes care of the inside of her home."

"Well I have good news. Then man I sent to Sanctuary has returned without finding you two. How did that happen?"

"I don't know." Michael said as he laughed. "We're both right there."

After a while Michael asked Bails about his two dogs. He loved them both very much.

"Oh I have both of them." Bails said. "I am buying a home out in the country and I'm sure that they will love it out there."

"So you're doing well I guess." Michael mentioned.

"I saved my money and built up my credit. Now it's paying off"

"Ha Bails." Evie said after grabbing the phone from Michael. How are you doing?"

Bails and Evie talked for a few minutes and then Bails said that he needed to talk to Michael again. Evie said her good-by's and handed the phone back to Michael.

"What's up?" Michael asked.

"I walked by the Colonel's office the other day and heard him talking to a Lieutenant Piles." Bails said. "I did some checking and found that this Lieutenant Randy Piles works for Army Intelligence at Fort Hood. When I walked back by a minute later the Colonel said "Just stay there and when you find them …" and that was all I heard. Although the man I sent has come back the Colonel might have sent this Lieutenant to Sanctuary to find you. I tried to get his picture but I couldn't find it."

"You're not going to." Michael said. "He's with Intelligence."

"I wouldn't go back to Sanctuary yet if I were you." Bails advised.

"We were thinking of staying right here." Michael said. "But I would like to get our tent and other things out of Sanctuary."

"I guess I could go by there and get it all." Bails suggested.

"I'll tell you what." Michael said. "I'll call Brother Mason and tell him to give it all to someone that can use it."

"I'm sure there is someone that can." Bails said. "Ha I need to go in case this phone is tapped. You two take care of yourselves." With that Bails hung up. He had no idea as to how long he was on the phone and hoped that it had not been tapped.

Bails' and Michael's phones had not been tapped but they could have been. The two men had to start paying attention or Michael and Evie could wake up some morning with twenty M-16's pointed at them.

A few nights later Michael and Evie were asleep in bed when they heard Maria screaming. Michael jumped up and threw on his shorts. He slept nude so putting on the shorts was a must. He ran out of the bedroom which was on the bottom floor. He ran around to the stairs and looked up at two men dragging Maria down the stairs. Two more walked behind them laughing. Michael did not want to step out until they reached the bottom of the stairs. Dropping her that far up might cause her to fall the rest of the way and kill her.

By time the men reached the bottom of the stairs the beast was ready. As soon as the two men dropped Maria the beast grabbed them both smashing their heads together. A large pool of blood on the floor proved that they were dead. The beast then grabbed the other two; one of which was able to break free and climb back up the stairs. The beast took the one he had and threw him against the wall also killing him.

From the top of the stairs the fourth man fired three shots from his pistol. Instantly the beast grabbed Maria and covered her with his shield. As the other man ran into one of the other bedrooms the beast held and looked at Maria.

Maria was scared at first but when she looked in the eyes of the giant beast that held her she saw a caring soul looking at her. She smiled and was no longer in fear. The beast lay her down at the floor by the stairs and stood looking at the top of the stairs. Then he let our a loud yell that shook everything around them and started walking up to where the bedroom was. Seconds later the fourth man screamed as he was thrown over the guard rail and to the bottom floor. With his head smashing against the front door frame he also died.

Then the beast went back to Maria who was being held my Evie by that time. He knelt down and looked at Maria. She saw the beast change back into Michael. She smiled and told them both that she loved them.

Maria agreed to have the four bodies moved to another place so that the police would not come there. Surely the Colonel would also come there and maybe capture Michael. Maria had heard all of the stories about the Neanderthal and now she knew that he was a good and loving creature.

Michael rolled the four bodies up in four large rugs that Maria agreed to loose. Then he put them in the back of a truck that Maria allowed them to use and took them off. It was still dark so there was no problem finding a dark place to dump the trash. When he got back he saw that there was a little blood in the back of the truck and washed it out. Then he came inside.

By this time Evie had Maria back upstairs in her bed. She was okay but there had been to much excitement for such an old woman. She was tired. When she saw Michael walk into her room she asked him to sit beside her. Then she wanted to hear his story. She wanted to know how a man could change into a Neanderthal.

Michael told Maria about how the government gave him alien DNA as a child and then Neanderthal DNA while he was in the Navy. Maria was amazed that her government would do this to it's citizens. Soon after finishing his story Maria fell asleep. Before falling asleep she did assure them both that they had a place to live for the rest of their lives.

The next morning everyone slept in late. For some reason none of them got much sleep that night. Finally they started to get up and move around. While Evie made a pot of coffee Michael turned on the TV. He usually only watched Fox News but in the mornings he did watch a local news channel to learn about any local news and see the weather.

The local news reported that early that morning four men were found dead and rolled up in rugs. It was believed that it was a gang war killing execution style. The four dead men were known members of a local gang.

"Good riddance." Maria said as she walked into the kitchen.

"Oh Maria." Evie said. "You shouldn't have come down the stairs by yourself."

Oh I'm okay." Maria assured Evie. "I need you to drive me to my attorney this morning if you don't mind Michael."

"Sure." he replied. "Anything you need."

After eating breakfast Michael changed into some nicer clothes and then brought the car around. Evie helped Maria out to the car and strapped her in. Then Michael took Maria to her attorney.

"Hello Miss Sanchez." the receptionist said as Maria and Michael walked in. "Is this your new boyfriend?" she joked.

"No." Maria replied. "He wouldn't be able to handle the action." Michael's face turned red as he blushed.

"Just go on in. He's expecting you."

Once Michael sat Maria in the chair in front of the attorney's desk he started to leave.

"Where are you going?" Maria asked Michael.

"What ever you're doing ... it is non of my business." he insisted.

"Oh but it is." Maria said and then ordered Michael to sit down. "This has everything to do with you and Evie."

Maria started by reminding the attorney that she had no family and that Michael and Evie were more like her kids than anyone ever has been. She said that she wanted to write a Will giving everything to them but with one stipulation.

"And what would that be Miss. Sanchez?" the attorney asked.

Maria turned to Michael and held his hands. "Michael ... I can see how much you two love each other. I am about to leave you two everything but ... neither of you get anything unless you get married. I don't like you two living in sin in my home."

"Well we have been thinking about it." Michael said. "But I still have to talk to her about it."

Maria turned back to the attorney and told him to add that stipulation in her Will. "But they must get married before I die and that may be any day." she turned to Michael and added; "So you two had better hurry."

The attorney typed up the Will and made sure that everything was correct. It took over an hour but he finally finished.

When Michael and Maria got back to the home Evie ran out to help Maria. When they got in the home Maria wanted to sit at the dinner table. She wanted some ice tea.

"You don't want any ice tea." Michael was sure of himself. "You just want to be here when I ask her."

"Maybe." Maria said with a big smile.

"Ask who what?" Evie looked puzzled.

"Maria had a Will written up ... giving everything to us." Michael said.

"Oh Maria." Evie yelled as she hugged Maria.

"But there's one stipulation." Michael added.

"That's right." Maria added with a big smile.

"You're not going to make this easy for me are you?" Michael asked Maria.

"Nope." Maria said still smiling.

"What stipulation?" Evie asked.

"We have to get married." Michael said looking at the floor.

Instantly Evie got excited and started to jump into Michael's arms. Then she suddenly stopped. She wanted to milk this for all she could. "I don't know. After all … no one has asked me."

"You're living in my home in sin too." Maria reminded him.

"That's right and we can't keep that up." Evie said. "Maybe you should move into one of the other rooms."

"Maybe I will." Michael said through his teeth. "You're not making this easy for me either are you?"

"Nope!" Evie said as she continued to smile. Maria was even laughing.

"Okay then." Michael said as he grit his teeth. "Will you marry me?"

"He didn't sound very sincere." Evie whispered to Maria.

"No he didn't." Maria agreed.

"Okay then." Michael said angrily as he turned and walked around the corner.

"No … Michael." Evie yelled as she started to run to catch him.

Suddenly Michael looked from around the corner and said; "Gotcha."

"You monster…" Evie said as Michael grabbed her and gave her a kiss.

"Will you marry me?" Michael asked with a big smile.

"I've been waiting a long time for you to ask me." Evie said as she gave him another kiss. "Of course I will."

"And don't worry about the cost. I'm paying for it." Maria insisted.

Over the next month Michael kept up his work taking care of the outside. On the other hand Evie was getting behind on some of here work as she and Maria worked on the wedding. Michael hated wearing a suit but it meant so much to Evie that he agreed to wear one.

Michael heard all of the jokes. There is a reason that a man wears black to his wedding. It is because he knows that his life is over. His bachelor party is really a good-by party from his friends. The groom gets drunk at his "bachelor party because he is realizing what he is doing. The grooms that do not show up at the wedding are the ones that have the balls to run.

The question came up as to who they should invite. Colonel Dillard was out of the question. In fact it would be better to not invite to many at all. Because they were non-denominational they asked Brother Gilmore to preside over the wedding. Of course Father Williams and Brother Mason would be invited along with Bails but they kept the invitations down to almost only them. They had friends at Sanctuary but the fewer that knew where they were the better.

To help Evie with keeping the home clean and with the cooking Maria hired three other women that worked under Evie. Without thinking Mason brought a woman to help him one day when he came to Maria's home. The woman that volunteered was Brady Willis. When Brady found out that Maria was looking for help she asked to stay there. She knew that Michael and Evie was there and wanted to continue her quest to win over Michael's heart.

That night Evie talked to the three women and recognized Brady for Sanctuary. She did not suspect anything was wrong and had no problem with her working there. On the other hand Brady had a problem with Evie. She knew that if they got married then winning Michael's heart would be close to impossible if not completely impossible. But she would have to be sneaky about it. She had to somehow cause Michael to start thinking bad about Evie.

The night that Evie met with the three women she told

Michael about Brady being one of them. He was surprised at hearing that Brady made it all the way to Maria's home. Then Evie told him how that Brady had come with Mason to help him but liked the idea of working and being employed.

One day UPS brought out a package for Evie. Brady answered the door but refused to sign for the package. She called Evie and then stepped over by Michael. When she saw Evie smiling at the UPS driver she made sure that Michael knew about it.

"Oh that's just Evie being Evie." he said. Then he looked up again as Evie put her hands on the driver's chest and joked with him. He dismissed it and got back to his work.

Brady was proud of herself. Although Michael had dismissed Evie's show of affection towards the drive the seed of doubt was still planted. Now she just needed to fertilize that seed and plant a few more seeds. Then maybe some day Michael would be her man.

Seeing Evie's hand on the UPS driver's chest and her getting close to him as she laughed bothered Michael more and more as the day went on. Finally that night as Evie took a shower Michael stewed over what he saw. When Evie came out of the shower he asked her about it.

"I'm friendly to everyone Baby." she said. "I don't even know the man."

"I would not have noticed it if ..." Michael stopped short of saying that Brady told him.

"If what?" Evie asked.

"It's not that important." Michael said. "I love you so much and I'm just scared of loosing you."

"You're not getting rid of me." Evie assured him. "I'm looking forward to a lifetime of torturing you."

Michael smiled. "I bet you are ... you and Maria."

That night Evie fell asleep in Michael's arms as she did many times. She loved falling asleep in his arms and he loved falling asleep holding her.

Although it was going to be a small wedding in Maria's home Maria was making sure that Evie had a beautiful white wedding dress. It took three weeks to make Evie's wedding dress and train. With the wedding just over two months away it seemed that everything was perfect. Then one day while Maria and Evie were making final adjustments to the train of the dress Brady walked in the room with a bottle of red wine and three wine glasses.

"I feel like celebrating." Brady said as she walked into the room. Then she tripped and the open bottle of wine spilt all over the train. It was ruined. With her hands over her mouth Brady pretended to be shocked at what she had done. "Oh my God." she yelled.

Evie tried to quickly jerk the train out of the way of the falling wine but she was not quick enough. She and Maria were shocked. There was no saving it.

"Oh my God Evie." Brady said. "I'm sorry."

"That's okay ladies." Maria tried to assure them both. "We still have nine weeks. I'll just have another one made."

"But I don't want to keep spending all of your money." Evie told Maria.

"Well look at it this way." Maria suggested. "Once you two get married and I'm gone it will be your money." Maria and Evie laughed.

"That's right." Evie agreed. "Spend away."

"What do you mean?" Brady asked.

"I put Michael and Evie in my Will but they get nothing unless they are married." Maria said.

Brady had just nine weeks to break the two up if she was ever going to have a chance at Michael. Now she began to form another plan but this time it included murder. However; she was no murderer so that plan would be put on the back burner until needed. But if anything else; if she could not get Michael and his soon-to-be money then Evie would not get it all either.

It took another two weeks to have another train made for Evie's wedding dress. By then Michael had his traditional black suit. He did not really mind the suit so much but the tie left him feeling like he was being hung. "Maybe I should be hung." Michael said to himself not knowing that Evie overheard him. "I'll be dressed for it."

Evie slipped her arms around Michael. "Oh my poor Baby. You getting those second thoughts?"

"Not really." he assured her. "It's more like stomach cramps." he added looking down at her with a smile.

"You are a monster." Evie told Michael as he jerked her around to face him. Then he held her tight and gave her a long kiss.

At that time Brady walked into the room. The sight of Michael holding and kissing Evie turned her stomach. "Well … Hello you two."

"Oh sorry Brady." Evie said. Michael gave Evie a last kiss and then went outside to work. Brady was cleaning the kitchen while Evie was cooking the evening meal. Evie was making her homemade chicken stew. Most people make chicken soup but Evie used large chunks of vegetables and cut the chicken up into large chunks as well. When it was finished Evie went into the dining room and set the bowls and other eating utensils on the table.

While Evie was setting up the table Brady was alone in the kitchen for a while; long enough to add her own spices to the stew. Then Brady came out into the dining room and helped Evie.

When everyone was called to eat they sat in their places. Evie took all of the bowls and filled them half way. When her bowl was filled she sat down. Maria insisted on praying over the meal before anyone ate. After the prayer everyone started eating.

Suddenly everyone was spitting back into their bowls. Evie looked around wondering what was wrong.

"I love black pepper Babe but this is to much." Michael advised Evie.

Evie took a small sip of the liquid from her stew and spit it back into her bowl. There was way to much black pepper in the stew. "It was perfect earlier." Evie told everyone.

Seeing an opportunity to look good by saving the day Brady ran into the kitchen. A few minutes later she came out with everything needed for making sandwiches. Brady did save the day and everyone still enjoyed their sandwiches.

That night Evie was thinking over what could have happened. Then she realized that she had left Brady alone in the kitchen for a few minutes. "She did it." she said out loud.

"Who did what Babe?" Michael asked.

"The stew was perfect until I left Brady in the kitchen for a few minutes." she told Michael. "She did it.

There was a knock on the bedroom door. "It's me ... Brady."

"Come in." Evie reluctantly said. "We're dressed."

Brady walked into the bedroom holding up a large can of black pepper. "While I was pouring the stew into the garbage disposal it jammed. This was stuck in it. Somehow the black pepper fell into the stew."

"Thank you Brady." Evie said. "That makes me feel better."

"Well now we know that it was not your fault." Brady assured her.

Then Brady left the bedroom and closed the door. Standing in the hallway she was proud of herself. She had not only made Evie look bad but she looked good. However; she only had six weeks left. That idea of getting rid of Maria before the wedding was looking better by the day. At least in that way Michael and Evie would not get all of Maria's money or her home. But not yet. She still had some time; a little time left. She still had six weeks before the wedding.

Chapter 10

Captured

The wedding was going to be on a Saturday so Bails had no problem being there. However; Brother Mason, Father Williams and Brother Gilmore had church the next day. Saturdays was also work day for those living in Camp McFarlin and Sanctuary. Brother Gilmore did most of his visiting the sick and older members of his church on Saturdays. They still promised to be at the wedding.

From time to time other things went wrong that made Evie look bad to Michael. One time she was running water in the kitchen sink allowing it to run down the drain as it warmed up. She stepped out of the kitchen for just a moment when she returned to the sink overflowing onto the kitchen floor. A wash towel had somehow fallen into the sink stopping up the drain.

At other times small parts of things for the wedding came up missing. Evie or Maria would lay something down but it would not be there minutes later.

One evening after eating supper Michael and Evie sat on a swing hanging from the second floor balcony. They loved sitting there slightly swinging as they watched the sun set behind the trees on the other side of the field. Suddenly a flowerpot fell from the balcony and smashed on the ground right in front of Evie's feet. If she had been getting out of the swing she would have been hit in the head.

Evie ran up to the balcony just outside Maria's bedroom and found no one around.

"What's wrong?" Brady asked. "I saw you running up here."

"One of these pots just fell and almost hit me." Evie told her.

"Yes. I know." Brady whispered to herself as Evie walked

back down stairs to Michael.

There was something in the back of Evie's mind that did not trust Brady. She did not know what it was but the feeling was strong. As she thought about it she realized that everything that had been happening lately had been happing after Brady came there. She talked with Michael and Maria about it but they did not see Brady as a problem. Evie dismissed the matter as just bad luck.

With three weeks before the wedding Michael and Evie went into town to eat out and see a movie. They asked Maria if she wanted to go with them but she just wanted to stay home. The ate seafood which was their favorite food. Then they went to the movie theater. While at the movie theater a problem came up where Michael almost changed.

Four members of the local gang called The Broods came into the theater looking to start some trouble. Michael and Evie were sitting in the tiny café inside the movie theater waiting to go in to see their movie. As Michael and Evie waited for the previous movie to finish so they could go in to see their movie the gang members came into the café.

"What do we have here?" one of the Broods asked.

"Back off little boy." Michael insisted.

"Ooooooo!" all of the Broods said as they crowded around Michael and Evie.

"Get out of the theater." a voice came from the entrance of the café.

The Broods looked up to see two police officers standing there. "The Popo." one of them said.

"You Broods are not allowed in the theater and you know it." the officer advised. "Now get out before we take you in."

"Okay Popo. Okay." the Broods left with a big smile on their faces but at least they left. Before leaving the head Brood looked at Michael. "Be seeing you later."

"You two okay?" the officer asked.

"Yes Sir … thanks to you two." Evie said.

"Well we had to do something." the officer said with a big smile. "It looked like your husband was about to take the trash out and burn it."

Evie grabbed Michael's arm. "It wouldn't be the first time."

"When you leave the theater be careful and look around." the officer suggested. "The Brood usually keep their word and that one said that he would see you later."

"I'm not worried about that punk ... or the other punks." Michael replied. "Gang bangers are nothing but cowards and trash. The government should pass a law that if you're found to be a member of a gang you'll be sent overseas and dropped in a hot zone. Then they can do all of the killing they want. But they are cowards to scared to face an enemy with an equal chance to kill them. They prefer attacking someone that can't defend themselves. All gang bangers are cowards."

"Well I do like how you think but ... the congress which would have to pass that law are all cowards too."

The police left the theater leaving Michael and Evie worried about the Brood that might be waiting outside. They watched their movie and then left. They found no one outside waiting for them so they got into the truck and came home. Michael was worried for Evie. Nothing would have pleased him more than allowing the beast to burn more trash.

A week later Evie asked Michael to go into town and get some tiny wire used to hold plants up. She needed it to hold up some artificial flowers for the weeding. Michael went to a local place called Ray's Gardens. Ray was a man that used to live at Camp McFarlin when he was homeless. With a small VA loan he was able to start his garden supplies store. Because he and Michael had been homeless at one time they got along well.

"Well good morning." Ray told Michael when he walked in the front door of the store. "What'cha need today?"

"Oh Evie needs some of that green wire used in holding up plants and vines."

"Got it right here." Ray said as he turned and took a roll of the wire off of the wall behind him.

Michael paid for the wire and was about to leave when he heard a familiar voice. "Well look-see who we have here." It

107

was the leader of the Broods that the police chased away from the movie theater. This time there were five of them.

"I don't need any problems here Guys." Ray told them.

"Isn't he cute." Michael said as he looked back at Ray. Suddenly something hit him on the head and knocked him out.

Later Michael woke up tied to a chair in some abandoned home that the Broods had squatted. He was still out of it and dazed. When he was able to gather his composure some he looked around.

"He's awake." some woman in the room said.

Seconds later the leader of the Broods walked over to Michael and slightly slapped him. Michael was still not even close to one hundred percent and did not even think about changing. He seemed to have no energy.

"Your cop friends chased us out of the theater." the leader said as others laughed. "Now you're gon'a pay for that. You see … no one treats us like that."

"The cops made you leave not me." Michael was barely able to say.

"You were with them and no one makes us leave anyplace." the leader insisted. "We left because we wanted to."

Michael was still so dazed from being hit in the back of the head that he did not realized that the leader flipped his knife open. Two women there ripped Michael's shirt open exposing his chest.

"Now I'm just gon'a have to cut you up some." the leader said. "I'm not gon'a kill you but that pretty woman might not want you anymore.

Michael half way knew what might be going on but he was still not fully alert. That was about to change. The leader lay the blade of his knife on Michael's chest and started to slowly cut. The pain was so great that Michael yelled out loudly.

As Michael changed into the beast the ropes and duct tape holding him in the chair broke. As soon as he stood he started grabbing Brood members and throwing them against walls. He grabbed one of them and literally ripped his head off. Grabbing one of the women by her arm he jerked her arm off at the shoulder and started using her arm like a club. By time the beast was finished he had killed seven of the Brood members but another six ran away. The beast walked out the back door of the home and saw the other six standing there. Letting out the loudest yell ever he ran towards the six. One of the men and one woman passed out. The beast stopped and looked at the man that had passed out and then ran away.

The beast ran into a park and climbed into a large drain culvert. There he changed back into Michael. He looked at his chest and saw that he had a scare but the cut had healed. Michael just sat there for many hours. Then finally he realized that it would be best to go back to his friend's store while it was dark.

By morning he had reached Ray's store. He went in the back door and found Ray still laying on the floor. He was still alive but still on the floor. Michael knelt down by his friend and picked up his head.

"I'll be okay my friend." Ray told Michael. "They only beat me up some."

"I killed a few of them." Michael said.

"Yeah … I saw them hit you in the head and then carry you away." Ray was more concerned about Michael than himself. "Where did they take you?"

"To some home where they were going to cut me up some." Michael told him. "I'm okay now."

Sirens could be heard getting closer. "I can't let the police find me Ray." Michael said as he lay Ray's head back down.

"I'll be okay." Ray assured his friend. "You get out'a here and call me in a few days."

As cops jumped out of the cars Michael stood and ran out the back door. Suddenly he stopped to keep from knocking someone down. It was another cop that got a good look at Michael's face. Michael continued to run. He would come back for the truck later.

As paramedics worked on Ray the cops were asking him who the man was. "He's just a man that stopped to help me." Ray was not going to tell them who Michael was. "He saved my life last night when the Broods came in and attacked me.

"It was the Broods that did this to you?" one of the police officers asked.

"Yes Sir." Ray insisted. "A lot of them came in here and tried to rob me but that man saved me."

"How did one man stop all of them?" the cop asked.

"He just started kicking ass." Ray said with a big smile. "Then he stayed with me all night in case some of them came back."

"Why didn't he call us?" the cop asked. "Some old woman walked by this morning and called this in."

Ray thought for a moment. "I don't think he was overly smart but he did save my life. That's all I know and that's all I care about."

Michael hung around in a large group of trees until the police left. Then he went to his truck but kept looking around in case the place was being watched. He got in his truck and drove back to Maria's home.

When Michael pulled up to the back door of the home Evie ran out to meet him. He was still weak so Evie helped him into the home and lay him on their bed. Maria walked in with a glass of ice tea but the tea was for Michael.

"We saw on the TV this morning that Ray's place had been attacked by the Broods. Maria told Michael. "Were you there?"

Michael told them both what happened and how that he had killed about seven of the Broods. As he talked Brady stood quietly in the hallway listening.

"*So you're that thing ... that Neanderthal.*" she whispered. Now how could she use that to help herself out? It would not do her any good if he was captured. Then again the reward had been raised to two hundred fifty thousand dollar. If she had a quarter of a million dollars then she would not need Michael. With the three in the bedroom not even knowing that Brady had been listening she walked away to make a phone call.

About thirty minutes later three police cars drove up to the front of Maria's home. When Maria answered the door the police pushed their way past her as one of them showed Maria the arrest warrant.

A few minutes later an ambulance drove up and the paramedics brought a gurney into Michael and Evie's bedroom. Michael was still to weak to walk. A few minutes later the gurney was on its way to the front door of the home with Michael on it. When he was in the ambulance it left with two of the cop cars close behind.

Maria and Evie were being held in the bedroom. The cops would not allow them to even go to the front door with Michael. Evie was raising hell but got quiet when she was threatened of being charged and taken to jail. "Take me to jail." she said just above a whisper. "I'll be with Michael."

"No ma'am." a cop said. "He's on his way to the hospital."

The cops started asking Evie and Maria questions about Michael. Suddenly neither woman could remember anything. When they refused to answer their questions they placed the twowomen under house arrest. Then he and the other cops left. One cop was left there to make sure the woman obeyed their house arrest.

That night Maria and Evie walked out on the balcony to talk. Maria asked the three women working under Evie to join them. As the five women sat at the table they talked about Michael.

"If he is the man that they have been looking for then he is worth two hundred fifty thousand dollars now." one of the women said.

"How do you know that?" Evie asked her.

"It was on TV last night." she said.

"Yeah it was." Brady added with a big smile.

"What are you smiling about?" Evie asked her.

"Oh nothing." she said. "I was just picturing how that much money was going to ... I mean how that much money would help."

Evie had a anger building in her but kept it from showing. *Could Brady have turned Michael in for the reward? Would she do it? How would she know that they were looking for Michael anyway?*

After a while everyone went back to their bedrooms except for Evie and Brady. As they stood close to the edge of the balcony railing they talked. Evie noticed a slight snicker from Brady every now and then. Finally she asked Brady what she was laughing about.

"Well what are you going to do anyway?" Brady said with a big smile. "I collect my money tomorrow and then I'm out'a here."

"What money?" Evie asked.

I was in the hallway this evening when you, Michael, and Maria were talking in your bedroom. I decided that I wanted the money more than Michael and made a phone call."

"You Bitch." Evie said. "We were finally going to be happy."

"Now I'm gon'a be rich and your not gon'a be." Brady said smiling right in Evie's face.

Evie lost it and hit Brady twice. The first time knocked Brady back against the balcony railing. The second one sent her over the railing to the ground. Brady hit the ground on her head breaking her neck.

"Stay right there." the police officer said with his finger pointed at her. He just walked around the corner of the home and saw Evie knock Brady over the rail. He checked Brady and she was in fact dead.

As Evie waited for the police officer to get up to the balcony she started crying. She and Michael were going to be so happy but now both of their lives were ruined.

"Miss Reilly?" the officer said. "Why did you knock her over the railing?"

Evie told the officer just who and what Michael was. Then she started crying again telling the officer that both of their lives were ruined. She just knew that she was going to prison.

"Well ... you do know Ray of the flower shop?"

"Yes." Evie said.

"Well ... he's my favorite uncle." the officer told Evie. "When I saw him at the hospital this evening he told me about the Neanderthal ... the big guy helped him and even saved his life." He looked at Evie and added; "So now I'm a fan of the big guy. You did ... probably what I would have done."

"What are you trying to say?" Evie wanted to know.

"I'm trying to tell you to stop crying." he told Evie. "I rounded the corner of the home after that woman hit the ground. When I looked up on the balcony I saw ... no one."

"You're not arresting me?" Evie asked.

"No ma'am." he told her. "Why should I? You didn't do anything wrong. But I do need to report this ... accident.

"What's your name?" Evie asked him.

"Peter." he said. "Peter Wales."

"Thank you Mister Wales." Evie said.

"It's Peter. Just Peter."

Peter called in the accident. When the ambulance and police got there Maria and the other two women joined Evie on the balcony again where she explained to them what happened. Later Peter was relieved and another police officer took his place. The ambulance took Brady's body away. Soon after that the police left except for the officer that relieved Peter. When the other two women went back to their bedrooms Evie told Maria everything that happened and what Peter did for her.

"Well ... we can't do much as long as we are under house arrest." Maria advised. "But in the morning I can call my attorney. I'm suing somebody." Evie helped Maria back to her room and helped her climb into bed. It was an exciting evening and she was very tired. Then Evie went to her own bed.

Evie did not like going to bed without Michael. As the night went on her anger grew but what could she do? Michael was wanted but she never understood why. He was wanted for being the Neanderthal but that was something that the government did to him. He had killed some people as the Neanderthal but the government was still responsible. Just after midnight she finally fell asleep.

He next morning the police officer told Evie and Maria that they were no longer under house arrest. They wasted no time getting to Maria's attorney. Once there Maria told him what all happened leaving out anything to do with the beast. The attorney did some checking and found out that Michael had been transferred to Fort Hood earlier that morning. About three hours later Maria and Evie were at the front gate of Fort Hood.

"Thank you Doctor." the gate guard said as he handed her ID back to her. "And who is this?"

"Oh this is my mother." Evie said.

Thank you Doctor." the guard said. "Go ahead."

With one guard behind them they still had the guard just inside the front door of the building to deal with.

"Hold it right there Doctor." the guard said as Evie and Maria walked into the building. Then he called Colonel Dillard.

A few seconds later the Colonel walked up. "You have an arrest warrant Doctor Reilly. What are you doing here?"

"For one thing you fat son of a whore, I do not have any warrant for my arrest. What I have is your desire to stop me and that is all. Second I am here to see my future husband. Now where is he?"

"Oh yes." the Colonel said. I did hear that you two were about to be married but … that will never happen now. Michael will be transported to a better facility tomorrow morning. In the meantime he is heavily sedated so he will not give usany problems."

"I take it that you mean that underground facility in Northern Oklahoma." Evie mentioned.

"Could be." the Colonel said with a big smile.

Suddenly Evie yelled out as loud as she could. "Michael … Michael. Where are you?" She remembered how voices carried through the entire building. "Fight back Baby."

With a wave of his hand two soldiers grabbed Evie and shut her up. "You're about to come up missing like he is." the Colonel warned her. "Now you two need to leave."

Maria grabbed Evie's arm. "He's right. We need to leave. Remember … live to fight another day. You cannot do that if you're arrested."

Maria and Evie left the building and Fort Hood. They returned back to Maria's home and talked about what they could do. They even discussed hiring Mercenaries to grab Michael on his way to Oklahoma. Maria had to money to do it so why not.

Chapter 11

God's Soldiers

Michael heard Evie yelling. He tried to get up but he was heavily sedated and could not move. He lay there trying to change into the beast knowing that if he could the sedation would leave his body. But he was unable to do anything. He knew that he was on his way to the underground facility in Northern Oklahoma and there was nothing that he could do about it. He also knew that if he was able to do anything it would have to be before he got to the Oklahoma facility. None of the others in that facility had escaped from there so he was sure that he would not be able to either.

Later that evening Colonel Dillard went to see Michael. Soldiers helped Michael to sit up on the side of his bed so the Colonel could talk to him. Michael sat there with the soldiers still having to hold him up.

The Colonel snapped his fingers in the face of the wobbling head of Michael. "Can you hear me Michael?"

"Yes ... Sir." Michael barely was able to say. "I'm sorry ..."

"That's okay Michael." the Colonel said. "How do you feel Michael?"

"Sick ..." Michael tried to look sicker than he was. "... like I'm gon'a throw up."

"Was laying down better?"

"Yes Sir." Michael was not pretending about this though.

The soldiers lay Michael back down. Then the Colonel continued talking to him. "You're going to be taken to place that can better assist you in this problem." the Colonel lied so Michael might not become combative.

"What's wrong with me?" Michael asked the Colonel.

"We don't know." the Colonel said still lying to him. "You

were arrested by a local police department and then they learned that you were wanted by us and gave us a call. By time we got to you, you were already like this."

"I'm … so sick." Michael was still acting weaker and sicker than he was.

"The nurse here is going to give you something to help you sleep." the Colonel suggested to Michael.

"No … no." Michael insisted. "It's making me sicker." Michael said as he felt a slight prick on his upper arm. It was to late to try anything then.

Michael knew then that he had been given more of the sedation. Now more time would be wasted sleeping it off. There was no way that he would be able to change into the beast while the Colonel was keeping him sedated.

That night Michael slept well only waking up one time after a dream. He had a dream in which he was in a hospital. Police found a 357 caliber pistol in the table beside his bed. The revolver had two 38 caliber rounds in it and one 357 caliber round. Then suddenly the pistol fired and Michael saw that one of the 38 caliber shells were spent. Then suddenly Evie walked up to him and got right in his face where she told him that she was coming to get him. Michael woke up wondering what the dream could mean.

"Father. If you gave me this dream then please explain it to me. Please help me Lord." Suddenly Michael fell asleep again.

Michael then had a second dream which seemed to be an extension of the first dream. In it he stood in a field full of flowers. Then a voice came from all around. "There will be three attempts to save you. The first 38 caliber round being fired represents the first attempt which has already failed. The second attempt will fail as well. But on the third attempt I will deliver you out of this."

Michael knew that God had sent the answer to his dream. He slept well the rest of the night knowing that God was in control. Later that morning the Colonel and a nurse came into

117

Michael's cell to give him an IV.

"Michael." the Colonel said waking him up. "The nurse here is going to give you an IV. You are severely dehydrated."

"No drugs." Michael barely said. "Making me sick."

"There's nothing in it but saline to bring your blood pressure back up." The Colonel was lying again. The IV was a way to feed him without having to wake him up to eat. There was also something in it to knock Michael out while he was transported to northern Oklahoma. Within an hour Michael was fully sedated and out cold. But things never work out the way they are planned.

Everything was put on hold when things started going wrong. This caused Michael's departure to be moved ahead four days. When Bails heard this he called Evie and told her.

"This never happens." he told Evie.

Evie told Bails that they prayed over this so maybe God was slowing down their trip to Oklahoma. Then she told him about hiring a mercenary group called God's Soldiers. Bails loved the news and had heard of them. According to Bails God's Soldiers had never lost a case.

Back at Fort Hood on the fourth day everything was set to transport Michael. With the IV removed Michael was placed on a gurney and taken to a military ambulance. Other than the driver the humvee had three armed soldiers which drove in front of the ambulance. A personnel carrying truck drove behind the ambulance holding twenty more soldiers. At 0700 hours the convoy left Fort Hood.

The day that Maria and Evie went back to Maria's home they talked about what they could do. When someone knocked on the front door Evie answered it. It was Peter. Evie let him and even gave him a hug. Then they walked out on the patio below the balcony and sat down. Maria told him what they were talking about and also mentioned hiring a mercenary group to help. The problem was that they had no idea as to how to contact any mercenary group. That was when Peter said that he knew of one.

They were called God's Soldiers. They were a group of Military Veterans and Christian men and one woman that specialized in helping Christians. Peter 1 knew how to get in contact with them. The three prayed asking God to see that the members of God's truth was not already busy and had time to help them. Peter left for his home where he had their phone number hidden.

When Peter left Maria and Evie got excited. The best thing about God's Soldiers was that they were based out of Dallas. Later that evening Bails called Evie. God's Soldiers would be at Maria's home the next morning.

It was a long night as Evie was waiting to meet God's Soldiers. She thought that Michael was probably already on his way to Oklahoma so time was wasting. By three in the morning Evie went ahead and got up. After making coffee Maria also got up. She could not sleep either. The two women talked for a while before the other two women joined them. So many people already knew that Michael was the beast that they decided to go ahead and tell the other two women. This way they might help.

One of the women admitted that she thought that Michael was the man that was wanted by the military but she was not sure. She overheard Brady talking to herself about it. Finally the sun started coming up. About an hour later Bails drove in with three pick-up trucks behind him. Evie ran out to give Bails a big hug.

"Is this them?" she yelled. "Are you guys God's Soldiers?"

"I'm Colonel Briks ... the commanding officer of God's Soldiers." The man said.

The Colonel's men waited outside as he fallowed Bails and the two women into the kitchen. They sat down and Evie began telling Briks her story. When she finished Briks just stared at he for a few seconds.

"So he is that Neanderthal we have been hearing about?"

"Yes and we were going to get married in two weeks." Evie started crying. "Can you help him?"

"Yes but ... we need to hurry." the Colonel said. Then he

119

reminded them; "But first there is a matter of two hundred thousand dollars.

"I'll be right back." Maria said as she drafted two of the Colonel's men to help her.

A few minutes later the two men came back with Maria behind them. The men set three wooden chests on the floor.

"There's over one hundred forty ounces of gold." Maria said. "That should more than cover it."

The Colonel ordered the two men to take the three chests out to the trucks but Maria stopped them. "I'm not in the habit of paying someone for a job that they have not even done yet." she insisted. "Now do your job and then I'll pay you."

The Colonel looked deep into Maria's eyes. Finally a smile slowly formed on his face. "If you were just a few years younger."

"What would you do?" Maria was getting feisty.

"I'd probably sweep you off your feet and marry you." the Colonel said with a big smile. "I do like your spirited woman." Then he looked at the two chests and back at Maria. "As you wish ma'am."

The Colonel called in his men and started planning. One of his men went straight to his phone and Maria's computer at the same time. With his connection to Colonel Dillard, Colonel Briks asked Bails to help. Within an hour Colonel Briks had all of the information that he needed to form a plan.

The morning that Michael was moved the convoy drove to Interstate 35 and turned north. When they stopped at that intersection God's Soldiers hit them. Briks thought that the soldiers guarding Michael would worry about the many civilians in the area but that did not happen.

The soldiers in the personnel carrier piled out and began firing at Colonel Briks' men. They were more organized than Briks thought that they would be. Outnumbered at least four to one Briks had his men retreat. This attack cost Briks two of his soldiers; one wounded and one killed. God's Soldiers quickly left the area with their dead and wounded before the police got there.

Michael lay in the back of the ambulance listening to all of the gunfire. He knew that this was the second attempt to free him and that they would fail. He also knew that the third attempt would be when God would step in.

Colonel Briks refused to do anything unless Maria and Evie promised to stay at home. To many times he and his men would be doing something that they were hired to do and the people that hired them got in the way. Now; even though Maria and Evie were not there he still failed in his duty and this did not set well with him. With the convoy a few miles ahead of Briks he and his men had to catch up and try again.

Using their personal pick-up trucks God's Soldiers raced to catch up with the convoy. They finally caught up with the ambulance just south of Fort Worth. From there they just fallowed the convoy. Briks wanted to give Colonel Dillard a since of security so they would not make another attack until they were north of Dallas and Fort Worth.

Rather than driving straight through the city the convoy took the loop around. Just as the convoy turned back onto Interstate 35 north of the cities God's Soldiers moved into position. Briks took the lead and pulled up beside the Humvee while his men fallowed in two more trucks. When Briks gave the word over the radio all three pick-up trucks slammed into the Humvee and personnel carrier truck with the soldiers in the back.

The Humvee slammed into a concrete wall and came to a stop. Briks and two of his men jumped out and took the firearms from those in the Humvee. When the personnel carrier hit the concrete wall it flipped over the wall landing on it's side. By time the soldiers started climbing out of the personnel carrier Briks' other men had rifles held on them. Two other men opened the ambulance door and got Michael.

"Michael." one of Briks' men yelled. Michael raised his head.

The two men grabbed Michael and helped him out of the back of the ambulance and into their pick-up. Then they got in and pulled up to Briks. The other members of God's Soldiers got in their trucks and they all left with Michael in the second truck. The entire attack from start to finish lasted less than one minutes.

Maria and Evie sat in the kitchen drinking their ice tea. They had already been briefed by Colonel Briks so they knew what was going on. After the failed attempt Briks called Evie and told her what happen. Then he assured her that they would get Michael.

As the women sat there Evie's phone rang. "Miss Reilly?"

"Yes." her voice was shaky.

"We have the package and will make delivery in three days." Briks said.

"I understand."

Evie had already been instructed to reply in that way so that Briks would know that they were safe. Michael would be taken to a safe house and within three days one of Briks' men would contact her and Maria. All of this was in case Evie's phone had been tapped.

"Did you record all of that?" a General asked Lieutenant Yoi.

"Yes Sir." Yoi replied. "Colonel Dillard needs to be informed."

Evie's phone had been tapped but the codes that Briks had set up between him and her were not helpful. However; Evie knew that Michael was safe and she would be with him again in about three days.

God's Soldiers had leased a large home out in the middle of nowhere for the soul purpose of hiding Michael. The three pick-ups pulled around to the back of the home where Michael was rushed inside. He was taken to a bedroom where a medical team working for Briks was waiting.

Instantly the medical team got an IV in Michael's arm in order to flush the sedation drugs from his body. The rest of God's Soldiers took up positions to watch for anyone coming onto the property.

Briks knew that Evie and Maria would be fallowed when they were to go to Michael so he had a plan already set up for that. Three days after Michael was freed a member of the God's Soldiers drove up to Maria's home. He was dressed in civilian clothes. He took Evie and Maria to a few clothing stores where the women pretended to look around and do some shopping. The man from God's Soldiers was looking around to see if they were being fallowed.

When they went to a forth clothing store the man from God's Soldiers was sure that they were not being fallowed. However; Colonel Dillard had the satellite watching them. He knew that they would lead him back to Michael.

When Evie and Maria went into the forth clothing store they were walked to a back room where they had a change of clothes waiting for them. After changing their clothes the two women were taking out the back door and into a waiting car with tented windows.

The car drove around a while making sure that they were not being fallowed and then finally headed out of town. They drove to a home far out in the country and pulled around to the back of the home. Then Evie jumped out of the car and ran inside. The driver helped Maria to get inside as well.

The woman at Fort Hood that was watching Evie and Maria called Colonel Dillard and gave him the GPS location on the home that Evie and Maria were at. The Colonel thought it was so funny that they had chosen a home only about one hundred miles north of Fort Hood. Colonel Dillard got two companies of soldiers and headed out of Fort Hood.

Twenty personnel carrier trucks fallowed Colonel Dillard. He was not playing around this time. The last attack that freed Michael killed three of his soldiers when the truck flipped over the cement wall. Another seven were badly wounded. The Colonel was out for blood now. Finally they reached the home.

Ten of the trucks spread out about four hundred yard from the home surrounding it. The other ten trucks pulled right up to the home with the soldiers surrounding the home and rushing inside.

"Oh there you are." Maria said as she held up her glass of ice tea. "You must be that Colonel Dillard I have been hearing about for a while and laughing at for a little while."

The Colonel was so mad that he slapped Maria with the back of his hand knocking her out of her chair and onto the floor. Evie rushed to Maria's side.

"You really are the son of a whore."

"You're gon'a stop calling me that." the Colonel said as he kicked Evie in the face. Then he ordered his men to search the home.

"Michael's gon'a kill you for this." Evie said with blood dripping from her mouth.

"Oh I don't think so." the Colonel said. "I will have him so sedated from now on that his grandkids will not be able to walk straight."

Minutes later his soldiers came back and said that Michael was not there. "What?" He looked at Evie. "Where is he?"

"You loose something?" Evie said with a really big smile.

Back at Fort Hood a woman walked into the Satellite Room and shot the woman watching the monitor. The silencer on her pistol kept anyone from hearing the shot. Then she set an explosive in the satellite computer and walked out of the room locking the door behind her. Quickly leaving the building the woman got in her car and drove out of Fort Hood. In her hand was a tiny box with a switch and button on it. When she was farther down the road she flipped the switch to "Activate". Then with a smile she pressed the button.

The explosion took out the entire Satellite Room and destroyed the rooms on both sides. When the Colonel got word of the explosion he was furious. He ordered his men to arrest the two women but they just stood there.

"That's an order soldier." the Colonel yelled.

"We don't fallow your orders." one of the soldiers said. "We fallow his orders." the soldier said as he pointed at Briks.

"Well hello Colonel Dillard." Briks said. "As you think you are about to apprehend Michael you have been apprehended

124

instead."

"What are you talking about?" Colonel Dillard asked. "My soldiers will stop you."

"What soldiers are those?" Briks asked him.

"I think he means one of those trucks leaving for Fort Hood out there." one of Briks' men said.

Dillard looked out of the window just in time to see the last three trucks leaving the property with his soldiers. "You can't kidnap me." Dillard insisted. "I'm a US military officer."

Briks waved at one of his men and asked him to help Colonel Dillard to find a chair at the table. As Dillard sat down he looked up at Maria and Evie who were still smiling from ear to ear but saying nothing.

"Now Colonel Dillard ... your home address is 703 Dragon Street. I know that your wife and granddaughter are there right now. You ... my friend are going to do something for us and we are going to return that favor."

"What do you want?" Dillard asked. He was mad but he was more scared for his wife and granddaughter.

"You are going to back off your harassment of my friend Michael and in return your granddaughter will not be harmed. Oh and keep in mind that I know you have four other grandchildren. We know where they are as well."

"Why are you doing this?" Dillard wanted to know.

"Why are you persecuting Michael so much?" Briks asked. "He's a good man. You're just a control freak."

"So ... what is your answer Colonel" Evie asked as she continued to smile.

"I'll do it." Dillard answered.

"And if at any time all of your grandkids pop up missing and you or your soldiers come back here and grab Michael or Evie then I will open a whole world of hurt on you. Do you understand?"

"Yes." Dollard said against his will.

One of Briks' men drove Colonel Dillard back to his home and dropped him off. Colonel Dillard had no intentions on keeping his word. This whole thing had become a vendetta now. He was going to see Michael in the secured area in Northern Oklahoma if it killed them both. But for now he would back off a while and make it look like he was cooperating. In the meantime he had plans to make.

Chapter 12

The Wedding

The home that Colonel Dillard had surrounded was leased for just that reason. Michael and Evie would be living in the home that he was already at. Maria would be taken back to her home. Colonel Dillard had been outsmarted and had no idea where Michael was. Knowing that some day soon the beast would show his face again the Colonel would wait.

Michael and Evie had to give up everything they had at Maria's home. If anyone was to try to bring their things to their new home then they might be fallowed and Michael could be recaptured. Their wedding would have to be a smaller wedding with no white dress or any friends being there. The wedding was still set for another week from then. That had not changed.

Maria was taken back to her home. She kept the other two women there to keep the place clean and to cook her meals. She would not be able to attend the wedding as someone might fallow her.

Colonel Briks got his gold from Maria and continued to check on her every now and then as a friend. He would also check on Michael and Evie from time to time as well. He and Michael had become good friends.

Finally the day came for the wedding. Brother Gilmore still presided over the wedding with the two witnesses being Bails and Colonel Briks. Bails brought in a chocolate cake for the celebration after the wedding.

Evie was so upset about loosing her white wedding dress that just before the wedding she went back into their bedroom and came back out wearing white pants and a long T shirt. She had one comment about it.

"Now I'm dressed in my white and I'm ready for the

wedding night as well."

"Are you wearing a bra under that T shirt?" a red faced Michael asked her.

"Nope." Evie replied. "Like I said. I'm ready for tonight as well." A big smile came up on Michael's face.

No one there cared how Evie was dressed. She was happy and that was all that mattered. It is against the law for any minister to marry a couple without a marriage licenses but Brother Gilmore did not care. If a couple sleeps together one night and the woman uses the man's name in something then they are legally married anyway. This is Texas law. So Brother Gilmore just made the marriage legal in the eyes of God. He opened and closed the wedding in prayer.

Michael and Evie were finally husband and wife. The party did not last long and everyone left. Michael locked up the home and fallowed Evie up stairs into the bedroom. They did not come down until the next morning.

The home was located just outside of a small Texas town with a population of only one hundred twenty. Michael had to grow his beard and mustache back so no one would recognize him. Evie died her hair red and kept it cut short. Everyone that knew her only knew her with long hair.

Michael continued to do well in controlling himself and not changing into the beast. No one in and around that small town knew who Michael and Evie were. They made many friends but after discussing it they agreed to keep a low profile. If they did anything that might draw attention to them then that might cause Michael to be discovered.

One day Colonel Briks came over and talked with Michael and Evie. Maria had passed away. She had hired Briks to make sure that Michael and Evie got their inheritance. They could not go to Maria's funeral. Surely Colonel Dillard would try to locate them at her funeral.

As Briks set up a meeting with Maria's attorney to read her Will he paid attention to only the attorney knowing about the meeting. He told the attorney that the meeting had to remain a secret because someone was trying to kill Michael and Evie both. The attorney understood and had no problem with the secrecy.

Briks was also mentioned in the Will so he had to be there as well as Michael and Evie. Come to find out Maria had more money than anyone thought. She had changed her Will to add Briks in it as a reward for the help he and his men did. She left him the home and property. This gave God's Soldiers a single place to live; a base of operation. Michael and Evie got just over one and half million dollars which included over half a million in gold and silver.

Michael and Evie's home sat on ten acres of land and was about fifteen miles west of Maria's home so they visited each other a great deal. As a friend Briks continued to help Michael with security at their home and on their property.

One morning Evie went to the doctor. She had been getting sick on most mornings. When she came back home she found Michael on the computer. She sat beside him and gave him some news.

"I found out why I have been getting sick in the mornings." she told him.

"Why is that Babe?" Michael was deep in thought.

"Well ... it's called morning sickness." she told him.

"That's probably right." Michael said. "I guess you would call ..." The words Morning Sickness finally hit him. He turned and looked at Evie but could not say anything.

"I'm gon'a have a baby." she told him.

Without getting up Michael hugged Evie. He was happy but also worried. He did not express any concerns over what might happen if he was caught again. *Would Colonel Dillard also take the child? Would he lock up Evie and the baby as well? What experiments would he do to the child?*

Evie got up with a big smile on her face. She told Michael that the baby was due in early January. As Evie went into the kitchen to make a couple of sandwiches for them both Michael watched her walk around the corner. He now had another reason to worry about Colonel Dillard finding him. Briks had told him about the conversation he had with the Colonel and that the Colonel said he would lay off of Michael but, was he telling just another lie?

Later that morning Bails came by for a visit. Michael and Evie met him in the kitchen where they sat down and talked. Bails told them that ever since Colonel Dillard had promised Colonel Briks that he would stop harassing Michael he had been acting strange.

"I'm the one that he always chose to set things up but now he has been asking others to do it." Bails said. "He could be planning anything and I would not know it."

"Be careful." Michael told him. "If the Colonel suspects that you have been passing information on to us then something might happen to you."

"I don't think he would do anything to me but maybe transfer me out of the state ... or out of the country." Bails replied.

As the three of them talked Briks knocked the back door. Evie jumped up and gave him the good news as she opened the door for him. "So you're gon'a be a Daddy." he said to Michael.

"It sounds like it." Michael replied. Not wanting to talk around Evie he asked Bails and Briks to join him outside. Once outside Michael told them about his fears that Colonel Dillard might want the child; a three way cross bread between him, Evie, and the beast.

"I told him that if he messed with you again I would go after his wife and grandkids." Briks said. "I wouldn't really hurt his grand kids but he doesn't know that."

"You don't understand." Michael mentioned. "The Colonel gets something in his mind and that's it. Nothing stops him."

"Oh I'll stop him." Briks said. "I really do not think he will try anything right now. I scared him to badly."

Three weeks went by with no problems. Michael now had complete control over the beast and Evie was happier than she had been in years. Michael went into town to buy a few things including some lumber. He was trying to build a doghouse so he could get his dogs back from Bails. He thought that he might never see them again but with their situation looking more stable things were changing.

While he was at the nail and screw section of the lumber yard he was trying to decide if he should use nails or screws on the doghouse for Dog. He stood with a box of deck screws and was shocked to find a man standing right beside him.

"Excuse me Sir." Michael said before he realized who the man was. "What are you doing here?"

"I'm just passing through but what are you doing here?" Colonel Dillard asked.

"None of your business." Michael insisted. "Now answer my question."

"Like I said." the Colonel said with a smile. "I'm just passing through. I thought I saw you over here and walked over to see if it was in fact you."

"You're suppose to stay away from me." Michael reminded the Colonel.

"No!" Dillard said. "I'm not suppose to harass you or try to grab you anymore. Look around. I have no soldiers with me except for my driver."

Michael stepped back and looked around. "What are you doing here ... in this store?"

"I needed some tape and that's all." Dillard calmly said. "Call your Colonel Briks if you want. After I get my tape I'm still leaving."

"Then get it and leave." Michael was not trying to be nice.

"I wish we could have got along." Dillard told him.

"We were until you started playing God."

"I told you then that I was fallowing orders." Dillard advised. "I was ordered to get you to that underground facility in Oklahoma. I fallow orders given to me."

"I still would not mind telling you things if you could just not ... fallow your orders so much." Michael advise Dillard.

"I almost lost my rank because of loosing you." Dillard said. "If we could make an agreement to meet every now and then ..."

131

"No deal." Michael interrupted. "I don't trust you anymore.."

"How is Evelyn?" Dillard asked trying to change the subject.

"She's just fine."

"Did you two ever get married?"

"Finally … no thanks to you." Michael said.

"You two plan on having a family?" Dillard asked.

Michael smiled. "She's pregnant now." he said not realizing that he was giving Dillard information he needed.

"Here's my card." Dillard said as he handed the card to Michael. "Call me if you would like to start helping again."

"Small chance in that happening." Michael said as he still placed the card in his shirt pocket.

"Okay then I need to go." Dillard calmly said. "It really was nice to see you again Michael."

"Yeah right." Michael smarted off. "Just get out'a here."

"Okay Michael." Dillard replied. "Take care of yourself and that baby."

That was when Michael realized that he had mentioned the baby to the Colonel. Now what was he going to do? Dillard might wait until the baby is born and then go after it. He would love to study the half bread baby that might have the same abilities as it's father.

Michael got his things and did not see the Colonel again; that day. When he got home he unloaded the truck and started working on building Dog a house. After a while he came into the kitchen and sat down at the table.

"Slow down Baby." Evie mentioned. Then she realized that something was wrong. "What's wrong Baby?"

"I saw Dillard at the lumber yard today."

"What did he want?"

"He said that he was just passing through and stopped for some tape." Michael advised her. "He had no soldiers with him."

"What should we do?"

"The first thing you should have done was call me." Briks

132

said as he walked in the back door.

"You scared the hell out'a me Briks." Michael said. "I didn't even see you drive up.

"I was in town about an hour ago and saw something that puzzled me." Briks said. "I saw Colonel Dillard walk out of the lumber yard store and you walk out a minute later. Now what the hell is going on here?"

Michael told Briks what happened while Evie got everyone a glass of ice tea. Briks did not think that Michael should worry as much as he was but Michael was more worried about the baby. When he said that Evie started to worry.

"Oh my baby." Evie said as she sat down.

"Stop worrying everyone." Briks insisted. "The Colonel had no soldiers with him and therefore was not looking for either of you. Now calm down."

"He gave me this in case I changed my mind about talking with him." Michael said as he tossed the Colonel's business card on the table.

"You haven't called him have you?" Briks asked.

"No ... not yet anyway." Michael advised.

"Don't do it." Briks advised. "If you do then he will find your home using the GPS on your phone. Then he might come with his soldiers and get you ... again."

"I never thought of that." Michael said. Then he got an idea.

Briks and Michael went back to the home that Maria had given to Briks and his men. From there Michael called Colonel Dillard and told him that he just wanted to let him now that he was reconsidering his offer. He told the Colonel that he would get back with him later. After hanging up he left he phone there at Briks' home. At least one of the members of God's Soldiers stayed with the phone to watch for any activity from Colonel Dillard.

Briks and Michael went back to Michael's home and did some more talking. For now it was a matter of waiting to see if Dillard was doing what Briks thought he was doing. If Dillard showed up at the God's Soldiers home then they would know that he was still trying to get Michael. But with the phone call being made from the God's Soldiers' home or; the Compound as they called it, then Michael and Evie would be safe.

Two days later Michael finished the dog house for Dog. Bails would bring the dogs back to him that evening. Michael took a bath and then sat down with more ice tea and waited. His missed his dogs and hoped that they would remember him.

When Bails arrived that evening he let the dogs out of his car. Michael yelled their names and both dogs looked at him for just a few seconds. Then they ran to him jumping on him and knocking him over on the ground.

Evie walked outside and the two dogs turned their attention to her also knocking her down. Evidentially the dogs missed them as well. It was warming up outside but Michael and Evie took their tea out to the patio so that they could spend time with the dogs.

"Dog has grown a lot." Michael told Bails. "What have you been feeding them?"

As the three sat there watching the dogs play Michael told Bails about what he and Briks did with his phone. Of course this meant that Michael had no cell phone anymore. He would have to get another one. As they talked and watched the sun go down action was about to start at the God's Soldiers' Compound.

Just as Briks thought Colonel Dillard was trying to reenergize his statue in the military. He was still a Colonel but he looked very bad after loosing Michael. Now he thought that he had tricked Michael into calling him giving away his position. Now the Colonel knew where Michael lived or; he thought that he did.

Briks knew that the best time to attack anyone was at 2:00 a.m. so he had his men rested and ready to play at that time. The problem was that he did not know what morning the Colonel would attack if he even did it at all.

The Colonel had two companies of soldier surround the God's Soldiers' Compound. Briks' men spotted the soldiers surrounding the compound but stayed quiet and hidden. They would only come out fighting if fighting started. Suddenly soldiers forced their way into the home breaking down the front door. As Colonel Dillard walked into the kitchen he saw many of his men holding their M-16s on Briks who calmly sat at the table drinking a cup of coffee.

"Where is he?" Dillard asked Briks. "Where is Michael?"

"This is my home and your breaking into ... "My Home" just made this personal." Briks said through his teeth. "Now you and your men will leave or I will order all of them to be killed along with you."

"Who the hell do you think you are?" Dillard asked.

"My nickname is Death and I have found you." Briks said. "Actually I found your wife."

"What about my wife?"

"You broke your word to me Colonel." Briks said. Now your wife is or will be dead. By now she is being held and my men are awaiting my word. If I don't call them in a few minutes they will assume that I am dead and then they will shoot her in the head." Briks stood and added; "I suggest that you leave as quickly as you can so I can make that phone call."

Colonel Dillard whipped around and ordered all of his soldiers into the trucks. Then they left for Fort Hood. Briks was not bluffing. He called his three men at Dillard's home and told them to leave. Dillard's wife was scared out of her wits but she was not harmed.

The next morning a soldier walked into Colonel Dillard's office and asked to speak with him. He was a sharp looking soldier with papers in his hand.

"May I speak to you Sir?"

"Of course but hurry up." the Colonel said. "I don't have much time."

"Well first thing ... Sir." the soldier said. "... if you do not listen to me your entire family will be wiped out starting with you right now." This got DillArd's attention.

The Colonel looked up and realized that this soldier was not one of his. "Who are you?"

"It does not matter who I am." the soldier told him. "What

does matter is that this is your last warning. If we even think that you are still pursuing Michael or Evie then we will wipe out your family … your wife, your children, and all of your grandchildren. Do you understand me?"

Dillard was mad. *How did this man get past his security*? Dillard was so mad that acting purely on instinct he opened his desk drawer and pulled out a pistol. Instantly the soldier pulled his pistol and fired three shots. The Colonel was only able to get off one shot but it killed the soldier.

Minutes later Colonel Dillard was being rushed to the base hospital. Two of the three rounds fired by the soldier hit him in the chest. The third round missed. Both of the bullets that his him passed through his right lung. He was badly wounded but he would live.

The next morning Briks went to Michael's home and said that his man had not returned from Dillard's office. He learned that his man had been shot and killed by Dillard but Dillard himself had been badly wounded and was in the base hospital.

"Well at least he won't be bothering you for a while." Briks said. "The problem is we don't know what he might have told others about what happened. The only person we have on the inside is Bails and I have not heard from him in days."

The two men continued to talk until Evie joined them. Briks told her about Dillard but she only wished that he had been killed. All they could do was wait.

That next Saturday morning Bails came out to visit Michael and Evie. He told them a few things but Michael stopped him. He wanted to call Briks and let him hear this as well. Less than an hour later Briks drove up and came in the back door. Bails began telling the others what had been going on. The shooting was being investigated by the FBI and the military but Dillard was saying nothing.

If anything Michael and Evie would be safe. Dillard only knew where the Compound was. No satellite was looking for anyone as the satellite Room still had not been repaired. It was being cleaned up but the computers and other things were not there in order to use the satellites. With Michael being the only; Changer as they called him and the others, still running free there was no rush to finish the Satellite Room.

It seemed that other than the investigation of the shooting nothing else was being done that Michael and Evie would have to worry about. Maybe the shooting finally got Colonel Dillard's attention. But it also got the attention of the FBI. Bails said that he would learn more the fallowing Monday. He would get back with Briks with any news every Saturday. If the news was very important then he would call Briks as soon as possible. However; Briks asked bails to call him every other day. If something happened to him then Briks wanted to know it.

Michael leaned back in the chair and let out a sigh of relief. Things might be coming to an end. He wanted nothing more than to see his child being born and not having to worry about Dillard. He even considered meeting with Dillard just so that he could kill him and end this. He might end up in prison or worse but Evie and their baby would be safe. Now even that plan was on hold.

Chapter 13

Dillard's Last Stand

Over the next month it was quiet. No one from the FBI came by the Compound asking questions. Everyone was finally settling down and taking it easy again. Evie was even happier if that was even possible. She was not showing yet but she had already started wearing clothing for pregnant women.

The two women that had helped Maria before her death came to see Evie. They were hoping that she might hire them. After talking it over with Michael they did just that. Jane and Deloris had a job again. With Evie being pregnant she would be needing help with the big home anyway.

Their home was not as big as Maria's home. There was only one bedroom on the bottom floor but two more on the second floor. Deloris took the bottom floor bedroom and Jane took the room beside Michael and Evie. Both women were young and full of energy. They would be very helpful to Evie. Michael felt better having Jane and Deloris there helping Evie.

One morning while Michael was in town he noticed that Ray's Garden Shop was open. He pulled in and found that Ray was back to work and his business was doing well. When Michael walked in the door Ray ran to him and gave him a hug.

"Good to see you my friend." Ray told Michael. "Where have you been?"

"To much has been going on." Michael; told him.

"Did you two ever get married?" he asked.

"Oh yes and I just found out the other day that Evie is pregnant."

Ray pulled a long steam red rose from his showcase. "Please give this to the new mother and tell her it is from me."

"I'll do that." Michael promised as he took the rose.

The two men talked for a while. Ray also wanted to know how the beast was doing. Michael only said that he had not seen the beast in a long time.

"You can control it?" Ray asked.

"I do now." Michael advised. "Just had to learn how."

Ray looked down and said; "Thanks again for helping me that day."

"Yeah I ended up … I mean the beast ended up killing about seven of them." Michael told Ray. "There's only a few of the Broods left now. I don't think they will be bothering you again."

"I read in the paper that seven of the Broods were found dead in an abandoned home." Ray said. "Everyone I know was happy to hear about that."

The two talked for a while. Then Ray saw some customers so he had to get back to work. Michael had a few things to do as well so he left. His next stop was the lumber yard again. He was installing security lights in the back yard. To many times Michael got up well before daylight and sat at the table in the kitchen drinking coffee. Anyone out in the back yard could shoot him and he would not even know that they were even there.

Again; the lumber yard was the place to go. Michael walked in and looked around. After finding the lights he looked for one that had movement sensors. He needed four that help two flood light bulbs each. Then he bought the eight bulbs that he needed and the electrical wire to connect them all and get them working. During his time in the store he kept expecting to round a corner and see Dillard standing there but the Colonel was at Fort Hood.

As Michael got into his truck to go home he heard a woman screaming. Looking up he saw three men grabbing the woman and trying to force her into a car. Then he heard the bank alarm going off. There was no time. If he was going to help then he had to move quickly.

A few feet away from Michael's truck was a large dumpster. He stepped behind it and crouched down so that no one would see him change. Then he changed as quickly as he could. He had learned that the quicker he changed into the beast the more it hurt. It had to do with the body stretching so fast.

The beast stood behind the dumpster and looked across the street at the three men and woman. By this time they already had her in the car and the last man was getting in. As the driver started the motor the rear end of the car lifted off of the ground a few feet. As the driver gunned the free spinning back wheels the beast tossed the rear of the car to the left. The car took off and hit a large tree stopping it. The beast opened the back passenger side door and got he woman out. As soon as he let go of her arm she ran back into the bank. Now it was time to turn his attention to the three bank robbers.

The beast began to smash in the roof of the car. Both men on the driver's side got out but the other man was trapped as the car roof continued to get smashed in. The driver took a shot at the beast but the bullet ricocheted off of the invisible shield. The beast roared so loudly that one of the windows in the front of the bank shattered. The other two bank robbers turned just in time to see the police driving up with their lights flashing.

"On your faces." an armed bank guard yelled. The robbers had surprised him before robbing the bank but never thought of taking his pistol. As the security officer held his pistol on the two bank robbers he looked at the beast. "Get out'a here. Hurry."

The beast turned and ran into the woods where he hid until it was dark. Only then did Michael come out and look around. Seeing no one around he got in his truck and drove home.

"You okay Baby?" Evie asked as Michael walked in the back door. She walked up to him and put her arms around him. She that something was wrong.

"I stopped a kidnapping tonight." Michael advised her. Then he sat down and told her what happened. Later they went into the den and sat in front of the TV and turned it on.

This time they watched the local news. Fox News would have to wait a while. It did not take long for the local news to tell a story about how a bank robbery was spoiled by what some of the people there was the Neanderthal.

"He came running across the road and picked up the back of their car." a witness told the reporter. "He was big. He got the kidnapped woman out of the car and then let her go. Then he started smashing that car."

"Well there you go folks." the reporter said into the camera. Our little town has been visited by the giant Neanderthal. And as usual there are no pictures."

The reporter signed off and went back to her van. A young lady stepped up to her and asked how much she would pay for a picture of the Neanderthal. Then she showed the picture that she took with her cell phone. The reporter called her boss and a deal was made for the picture.

The next morning the picture of the Neanderthal tossing the car to the side was all over the airways. Even Fox News had a copy of the picture.

"Thank God they did not get a picture of you changing." Evie said.

"I was not going to do it but there is no telling what they might have done with that woman." Michael tried to defend himself. "What was I to do?"

"I know Baby." Evie assured him. "You're just a big … lovable … teddy bear."

"Oh I am not." Michael tried to play it down. The truth was that when ever he saw something wrong he wanted to step in and help. But he could not do it much before when he could not control the beast. Now he could so what should he do?

Evie talked to him about becoming a realistic supper hero fighting crime. Of course she was joking but Michael did not know it.

"Supper heroes live in the city and I'm not moving into any city." he insisted.

Evie almost doubled over laughing. "I was joking Baby." Then she decided to play with this. "Then again … I could

141

make you a costume … a diaper. After all you are my Baby."

Okay Babe." Michael said with a smile.

As Michael sat down at the kitchen table Briks knocked on the back door. Evie ran over and opened the door.

"Did you hear the news?" Evie said with all of the excitement in her.

Briks thought that he was going to hear that Colonel Dillard was dead but that wasn't it. "What is it?"

"Michael is going to start fighting crime as a big Neanderthal wearing a diaper."

"Babe." was all that Michael could think of to say.

"You're what?" Briks asked Michael.

"I'm just joking." Evie told Briks. "I'm just joking."

Evie invited Briks to eat with them. She was cooking up a batch of smoked hog jaws and pinto beans and rice. She was mixing up the sweet jalapeño cornbread batter getting ready to pour it in the cast iron pot.

Briks sat down and Evie brought him a cold glass of tea. Just as he sat down Odie ran up to him and tried to jump up into his lap. Odie was getting older and could not do things like he used to do.

Michael showed Briks his security light setup for the back yard. It was okay if you wanted to light up someone that was about to do something but that was about it. It did nothing in stopping anyone. Briks suggested setting anti-personnel mines but gave Michael a serious look and hen started laughing.

"Unfortunately; this is all you can do." Briks told Michael.

Briks had already left Michael and Evie with a few firearms. They both carried a pistol on the property which is legal in Texas. They could not get CHLs or the government would know where they were. Michael also had a Ruger 10/22 rifle for hunting small game on the property.

The security lights, alarms, and firearms were the only security Michael could get that was allowed by law. Most people did not have this much but Michael worried about Colonel Dillard trying to grab their child. In his mind he could not get enough security.

It was early July and everything seemed to be going well. Michael and Evie were still making friends in the small town in which they lived. God's Soldiers had a few contracts where they made some good money. Even Bails had a new girlfriend and was thinking of asking her to marry him. But thee is always someone that can and usually does mess up any good times.

Colonel Dillard had healed up well. He had been going through therapy and was in better shape that he was before the shooting. Dillard had a private conversation with Lieutenant piles, the man he send into Sanctuary to find Michael and Evie. Dillard wanted to use him again but in a different way. He swore Piles to secrecy and then told him all about Michael and Evie. He also told piles about his interest in their child.

Evie was now four months pregnant but she had been showing forever ,month. She and Michael feared that the baby might get to big for a normal birth. They also feared what the baby might look like. This was something that they had no considered.

One day when Evie was seeing her doctor he sent the nurse out to get something. As soon as the nurse left he said; "Listen to me Evie. A Colonel in the military is forcing me to give allayer information to him and my nurse is working for him ... not me."

"Is the Colonel's name Dillard?" she asked.

"Yes." the doctor quickly answered. "That's it."

The nurse came back into the examination room so the doctor and Evie stopped talking. Before leaving the doctor's office Evie grabbed the doctor's hand and thanked him. "No Doc. Thanks for everything."

Evie was scared all of the way home. She could see Dillard in every car that passed her. She passed some kids playing basketball and she could swear that they were watching her. She was so paranoid and by time she got home she was a nervous wreck.

"Everybody was watching me." Evie told Michael as she shook from fear.

Michael called Briks and asked him to come over. Within thirty minutes he was walking in the back door.

"I'm getting tired of this Briks." Michael said. "I'm getting ready to take care of him myself ... on a permanent basses."

"Let us take care of this Michael." Briks advised. "But tomorrow we leave on a job and won't be back for about a week. This is a big job paying a great deal of money. Dillard isn't going to do anything during this week. Right now Evie's doctor is just fallowing orders from a corrupt government so don't get mad at him. Just play along."

"Okay man." Michael calmed down some.

"When we get back we'll take care of Dillard on that personal basses."

Briks left to get ready for God's soldiers' next job. Michael did what he could to calm Evie down. He even started walking around the property and the home carrying his pistol on his side. This actually worked in helping Evie to feel better.

Later that even a woman from God's Soldiers came to see Evie. "Hello Evie." the woman said. "I'm Sandy Perkins ... part of God's Soldiers' medical team. While they are on a job where no woman can be found I am suppose to take care of you. You are not to go back to your doctor until Colonel Briks gets back."

Evie agreed and then had Jane show Sandy the extra bedroom. Once Sandy got settled in she came back downstairs and gave Evie a complete physical. She also noticed that the baby was larger than it was suppose to be but did not alarm Evie about it. It was a concern but she did not want Evie to worry. If anything Evie might have to give birth through a cesarean. She also knew what Michael was and that this baby could also be part Neanderthal. With the size of the baby this was looking like a very good possibility.

Michael began working on a book about his experiences as the beast. In it he told many of the stories of what happened when he changed into the beast. It was mainly a collection of notes that he would put together later. He just wanted to let the American people know that their government does

144

experiments on them.

When LSD came out as a drug it was used by the American government in mind control studies. In these experiments they used hundreds of American citizens as their lab rats before moving on to experimenting with foreign spies.

Sometimes the population of whole towns come up missing. You never hear much about it because the news is shut down before it get out to far. But the news still gets out only to reach a few ears. Most Americans do not want to believe that their government would do such things and therefore shut their ears to it. This is exactly what the government wants.

Michael even allowed Evie to get in on the book. She was the one that put it together as a book speaking as a third person telling the story.

Michael and Evie spent the next week staying busy. As Michael continued to walk around the property carrying a pistol a UPS driver got the shock of his life. He dropped off a box in the front porch only to turn and find Michael standing there with his pistol hanging on his side. The neighbors on both sides of them stopped coming over to visit because of it but Michael and Evie did not care. Both neighbors acted like Liberal/Communist anyway.

Finally nine days later Briks called Michael and said that they were home and he would be there the next morning. Michael and Evie were excited to see what Briks had planned for Colonel Dillard. Evie was doing much better. She stayed busy around the home which helped her a great deal.

The next morning Michael got up well before daylight to work on his book. As he sat at the dinning table he noticed that all of he floodlights came on in the back yard. He grabbed his pistol and stood to the side in the shadows. Then he saw something he did not expect. A pick-up truck drove around into the back yard. It was Colonel Briks.

Briks did not usually come over that early but he could not sleep and he knew that Michael would be awake. Michael met Briks at the door and let him in. After Briks got his cup of coffee the two men sat down and began to talk.

"I was so wound up after our last job that I could not sleep so, I got up and got on the computer." he told Michael. "I also made a few phone callsand found a few things out."

"You call people this early?" Michael asked.

"In my business you might get a phone call at anytime for any reason." Briks mentioned. "It seems that Colonel Dillard may get a promotion if he can collect evidence that your child has the same abilities that you do."

"That kind of information would be top secret." Michael said.

"I have connections that are more loyal to me than Dillard." Briks said with a smile. "You would be surprised at how many people that work for Dillard don't like him."

"Not really." Michael said with a smile. "So what are you going to do about Dillard?"

"I can't tell you right now but by noon Dillard will comply with my wishes or he will be killed." Briks advised. "I'm tired of this man. Even if I did not know you I would go after him. He re-defines the words "Ass Hole.""

"And what is this going to cost me?" Michael asked.

"Not a thing." Briks said. "This one's on me."

"Well thank you." Michael was happy about that. "You were starting to get all of my money."

"You mean my money don't you?" Evie asked as she walked into the kitchen and got herself a mug of coffee. After sitting down at the table she asked; "So what's this about ... my money?"

"Yap!" Michael said. "I'm married."

The three sat there talking for almost two hours. At one point Evie had to get up and make another pot of coffee. When Jane and Sandy got up the three had to stop talking about what Briks was going to do with Dillard. As the two woman sat at the table Briks said that he had to leave. He had things to do.

As Briks walked out of the backdoor and outto his truck Sandy said; "God ... he's hot."

The others at the table started laughing but Sandy was

only about four years younger than Briks. She knew that he was married to his job so she would never stand a chance. But that was not the way Evie saw it.

Around 10:00 a.m. two of God's Soldiers; a man and a woman, knocked on the front door of Colonel Dillard. Dillard's wife answered the door and the two pushed their way into the home also pushing Dillard's wife back. With his wife on the floor the woman pulled her pistol and pointed it at her.

"Shut up and listen." she ordered Dillard's wife. "I'm not going to kill you but you are going to give him message. Do you hear me?"

"Yes." the scared old woman on the floor said.

"Does your husband love you and the grandkids?" the woman asked.

"Yes he does." she answered. "Why?"

"He has been threatened many times that if he continued to do what he was doing against a man we know something would happen to you and the grandkids." the woman with the pistol said. "Yet he continues so we are sending him a final message."

The woman aimed at the left leg of Dillard's wife and fired. The silencer kept it quiet. "Tell your husband that if he continues then we will kill you and all of the grandkids but we will leave him alive to know that you're all dead because of him. All he has to do is leave Michael alone and we will leave you all alone."

The man with the woman got the home phone and sat it on the floor beside the woman. Then he said; "Call your husband and tell him what happened but ... first call an ambulance."

"Why would you make it easy forme to call for help?" the woman on the floor asked.

"Because we don't really want to hurt you Miss Dillard. Your husband is forcing our hands."

The man and woman from God's Soldiers left the Dillard home. In seconds they were gone. Miss Dillard called 911 and got some help coming and then called her husband.

Colonel Dillard rushed home and found the police and an

ambulance already there. He wife was on a gurney and on her way out to the ambulance. The police wanted to talk with him so he promised his wife that he would be at the hospital as soon as he could.

"Colonel … do you who might have done this?" one of the police detectives asked.

Dillard thought for a moment. Who ever was there could have killed his wife and chose not to. He was mad and wanted nothing more than to grab Michael and Evie. However; this was getting out of hand and he was about to loose his wife and grandkids.

"I have no idea who would have done this." he said.

Colonel Dillard ended up giving up his attempts to grab Michael. Loosing his family was not worth it. He considered resigning his commission and getting out of the military but asked his superiors for a transfer instead. He got his transfer but was demoted back to the rank of Major.

Another man was promoted to the rank of Major and sent to Fort Hood to take over Dillard's job. He was Major Frank Gillis. Major Gillis was younger than Dillard; closer to Michael's age. He spent the first three weeks of his duty reading reports and talking to others about Michael and Evie. He was given unlimited power to capture Michael, Evie and their baby. The problem was that he had to find them first.

Briks learned and Dillard's transfer and about Major Gillis. He worried that his new Major might be more dangerous than Dillard ever was. One day Briks went to Michael to talk to him and Evie about a plan he had. After they talked Michael packed a bag with clothes to last at least a week. Then he left with Briks. A few of God's Soldiers would come help watch over Evie until Michael got back. With no more bedrooms they set up cots in the den.

Chapter 14

Wasted Time

Briks and Michael went back to the Compound to pick up two more of God's Soldiers. The plan was to travel around the southern part of the country and have the beast show himself. This should draw Major Gillis away from Texas. Their first stop was in Texarkana.

It was late in the night when they pulled into a wooded area close to a major truck stop. Michael got out of Briks' pick-up truck and changed into the beast. As the beast he was still unable to speak but he was able to understand what he was to do. It was simple. For their first act all he had to do was run through the parking area of the truck stop. Then he was to jump the back fence and run away.

The beast did as he was suppose to do until a driver pulled a pistol and fired. Being hit the beast stopped. This time he was hit in the side of the chest under his left arm. This was the last thing that Michael was expecting. The beast fell to his knees but he was able to extend his shield so he could not be shot again. The man ran up close to the beast and fired two more shots which ricocheted off of the shield. One of the bullets hit the driver in the leg.

The beast slowly stood as other drivers watched. He leaned over and picked the driver's pistol up and then threw it over the fence. Then he growled just before letting out a very loud low toned yell. With plenty of witnesses to say that he was there the beast jumped the fence and ran off just as planned.

Later that night Briks picked up Michael who was limping as he walked. When they got back to the motel room Briks found that the limp was caused by Michael twisting his ankle and not from him being shot. Although the bullet wound had healed the bullet was still inside his chest. It had to be removed.

One of the people with Briks was part of his medical team. Luckily he had brought the surgeon. Briks bought a bottle of whiskey for Michael. After drinking enough of the whisky Michael passed out and the surgeon started looking for the bullet. It took over thirty minutes just to find the bullet and another fifteen minutes to remove it.

The bullet had passed through the upper part of the left lung but the surgeon would need an operating room to fix that. On the other hand maybe Michael could fix it by changing into the beast and then back to Michael. The surgeon patched Michael up and waited until he woke up.

It took Michael just over three hours to start waking up. He had one big-time hangover. It was another hour before he could understand what the surgeon wanted him to do.

"Michael." the surgeon said. "Wake up Michael."

"What do you want?" Michael finally responded.

"Michael. The bullet passed through your left lung. I need you to change into the beast and then back to human form so it will heal. I cannot go into your chest to sew up your lung without an operating room."

"Okay." Michael uttered but was still to drunk to change.

"That's okay Michael." the surgeon said. "Go ahead and sleep it off. We can try again when you wake up."

Michael lay back down and groaned. The others in the room looked at each other and smiled. The surgeon, nicknamed Doc, said that Michael should be okay for a while. He was not bleeding from the mouth. It was another three hours before Michael woke up again. This time he was more responsive although he still had the hangover.

"The bullet went through your left lung Michael." Doc said. "I need you to change into the beast and then back to you so your lung will heal."

"I remember you asking earlier." Michael said as he sat up on the side of the bed. He sat there wanting nothing else but to go back to sleep but he knew that this was important. He concentrated and slowly began to change. A minute later the beast stood and looked around. However; as he changed back to Michael he collapsed onto the bed.

Doc looked Michael over and found that where he cut Michael in order to find and remove the bullet had healed. Surely the lung also healed. But they did discover one more thing. The alcohol in Michael's system did not leave his body when he changed into the beast or when he changed back. Then Briks remembered saving Michael from Colonel Dillard. He was heavily sedated and it took a while to get that out of his system.

"Evidentially; what ever chemical is in Michael's body before he changes into the beast never leaves when he changes back to human form." Doc suggested. "Bullet wounds and cut do heal but any bullet in his body also stay there. We now know that as well."

God's Soldiers and Michael drove on to Denver, Colorado. Once there they settled in for a few days. Michael was still a little tender from the removal of the bullet. Although the wound healed it was still tender and a little painful for a few days. After a few days Michael felt better and they decided to have another show of the beast.

It is not easy to find crime happening. One might think that it is but it is not. As God's Soldiers drove around with Michael they finally found a few gang members selling drugs at an old Mom-and-Pop store. Michael was dropped off two blocks down the street where he quickly stepped into the shadows of a building. Once hidden in the darkness he changed into the beast.

The beast ran down to the Mom-and-Pop store and grabbed one of the drug dealers. The others ran. Briks made an anonymous phone call to the police and told the dispatcher that the Neanderthal had grabbed some drug dealers and was shaking the man. Then he hung up. Within a minute three police cars pulled up. This time the beast was using his shield.

The police instantly pulled their pistols and pointed them at the beast. Realizing that the police saw him as a threat the beast dropped the drug dealer and ran. One of the officers fired three shots before stopping but the bullets ricocheted off of the shield. This time Michael was safe.

Briks wanted to wait another week before doing anything again. They drove to Seattle, Washington where they sat in a motel room for almost a week before doing anything. But before doing what they had planned to do Briks stopped at a check cashing business to cash a check. While he was inside Michael and the other two members of God's Soldiers sat in their two pick-up trucks. Then suddenly an alarm went off and police started surrounding the business in seconds. Not knowing what was going on the three just sat there and watched.

Three young punks were trying their first robbery and were not doing well at it. Instead of leaving when the alarm went off they stayed to get more of the money. Now they were trapped with two employees and two customers including Briks. Michael stepped out of the truck and walked up to where local people were gathering.

After a while two of the punks stepped outside with Briks. With a pistol pointed at his head the punks made a few demands. Then to show that they meant business they shoved Briks into the street and the one with the pistol shot him. Briks collapsed and did not move.

Michael had, had enough. He instantly changed into the beast and stepped out of the crowd. Only one little girl saw Michael change but the others there were shocked to see this giant beast step out from among them. *Where did he come from? How long had he been among them and they did not know it?* The beast just stood there as the two punks quickly got back inside the business.

The two punks saw the beast standing there looking at them. They were already panicking but this emotion only got worse with the beast watching them. The beast calmly walked over and picked up Briks. After bringing him back to where the crowd was he turned his attention back to the punks.

The beast walked back to the business and stood in front of the glass door. Bullets started flying through the door hitting the shield around the beast. This time the police lined up on both sides of the door. The beast was no longer the enemy. The beast looked at the cop to his right. The cop nodded his head and the beast nodded back. Then the beast walked through what was left of the glass door and stood inside. The police ran in on both sides of him and arrested the punks that just stood there frozen in fear.

Suddenly the beast turned and ran outside. After looking around he ran into a large group of trees. Once on the other side of the trees he changed back into Michael. Then he calmly walked far around so not to be noticed and got back into Briks' truck.

Their plans had to be put on hold while Briks was in the hospital. For a while he would also be in the police eye and the public's eye for the next few days. The two members of God's Soldiers had a new job now. Keeping Michael hidden was more important than anything else. As Briks healed and told history; what he wanted them to know, to the local media Michael had to stay in the motel room. Food was brought to him. After a week of this Michael started getting restless.

Briks was finally released from the hospital but he had to get a motel room by himself until he knew that he was no longer being fallowed by the media or police. After three days he met with Michael and the others and left town.

The local newspapers told a story about a Neanderthal that saved a man that had been shot by one of the thugs. Then police working with the Neanderthal arrested the thugs after which the creature ran off never to be seen again.

Briks took the small group to Los Angles, California. The first thing that they did was get a motel room to operate from as they had been doing. Crime was all over the city but finding something actually happening was another story.

One morning the small group was sitting at one of those Quickie-Marts with gasoline pumps filling their trucks when an opportunity presented itself. There was suddenly a loud sound of twisting metal as a big truck and two cars crashed into each other on the road in front of the pumps.

"Save the people." Briks said to Michael.

Michael got out of the pick-up truck and went behind the store. In the shadows of the building he changed into the beast. Then he ran around to the wreckage and literally ripped the door off of one of the cars. After tossing the door aside he pulled the old woman out and carried her a ways away to safety. Then he went back to the other car and tried to rip that door off but it was better built. He simply opened the door and pulled the young woman and her three kids out. He carried the woman to where he left the old woman but her kids were able to fallow on foot.

Suddenly the fuel on the road flashed on fire and the truck driver began to yell for help. The beast had to cross the flames to get to him but still being a wild animal he hesitated. As the flaming fuel slowly ran closer to the driver the beast closed his eyes and lifter his hands towards the truck. His shield extended out in front of him and pushed the truck which began to slide away from the flames. Other bystanders were able to free the driver. With everyone safe the beast turned and ran off into some trees close by. Some people tried to fallow him but he was lost.

About three hours after the beast saved the day Briks drove up beside Michael who was walking down the road. The four went back to the motel room where they cleaned up and rested. Briks was happy with how things turned out.

Not one person died in the wreck thanks to the beast. However; only one newspaper reported how that a large Neanderthal saved the lives of three adults and three children. The liberal bias media on the television told a story of how this Neanderthal almost killed everyone with one Television station even blaming the whole accident on the mysterious creature.

As they watched the media telling their usual lies of the story Michael just wanted to get out of the area. All the beast ever did was help people but as long as the liberal bias media had cameras the truth would never be told.

Briks and the others stayed at the motel for three more days waiting for the news about the "deadly" creature to die down. Then in the middle of the night they left town and headed east.

While the other two of God's Soldiers drove along the east coast the passed out pictures of the beast doing different things. It was their job to make it look like the beast was along the east coast when in reality Briks and Michael went home. They had been gone for almost a month so Evie was happy to see Briks' truck drive up to the back door.

Evie was now five months pregnant and showing a great deal more than she was when Michael left. When Briks and Michael pulled around the back of the home Evie get up from her chair at the kitchen table and ran outside. For a long while Michael and Evie just held each other.

"Get a room you two." Briks said with a smile.

Then Sandy came outside and walked up to Briks. She did not want to come on to strong but she was happy to see him as well. To her surprise Briks grabbed her hand and the four walked into the kitchen and sat at the table. Sandy scooted her chair close to Briks.

"Have you two guys been watching what this Neanderthal has been doing?" Evie asked as she laughed. "That Neanderthal is getting around."

Evie had the TV turned to the local news and at that time another report came in about the beast. This report came out of Saint Louis, Missouri. The reporter had a picture of the Neanderthal running across a Walmart parking lot. The Neanderthal was reported to have done nothing but run across the parking lot.

Evie and Sandy looked at Michael and Briks. Then the two men started laughing. Finally Briks told the women about him having two men driving around the country dropping off pictures of the beast.

Michael and Evie left for some "alone" time leaving Briks and Sandy sitting at the table alone. For a while Briks and Sandy talked and then realized that they were both interested in each other. Briks was about twelve years older than Sandy but she preferred older men anyway. They agreed to go out that night.

By time Michael and Evie came out of the bedroom Briks was already gone and Sandy was cleaning the kitchen. Sandy wasted no time grabbing Evie's hand and sitting her down at the table.

"Dan asked me out tonight." Sandy said. She was excited.

"Who is Dan?" Evie asked.

"Dan." Sandy replied. "Dan Briks." No one knew Colonel Briks' first name.

The women talked for a while and then Evie gave Jane and Sandy the rest of the day off so that Sandy could get ready for her date. Letting only Sandy off work to get ready would not be fare to Jane so Evie let her off as well.

After a while Sandy started getting ready while Evie walked over to Michael. He was on the computer writing in his book. He was adding the newest adventures of the beast when two hands slid around his neck and someone gave him a hug.

"God ... I hope that's you Babe." Michael uttered as he continued to type.

"Well just who else would it be?" Evie quietly whispered.

"Well Brady used to ..."

"She used to do what?" Evie said out loud as she quickly stood.

Michael whipped around and grabbed Evie holding her close. "Nothing ... nothing." he assured her. "I was just picking."

"You had better be." Evie ordered."

A few minutes later Evie left Michael to his book and she went to see if Sandy needed any help. The two women talked while Sandy got ready for her date. Dan was like Michael in that he did not like a woman wearing a lot of make-up so she had to keep it toned down some. For some reason some women think that they have to apply their make-up with a steam shovel. They look more like clowns than women.

Around 6:00 in the evening Briks drove around to the back of the home. He came in and got Sandy. Michael and Evie saw them both off remembering their first few dates. After Briks and Sandy left Michael and Evie went into the den to watch the

TV. Looking for a good movie they came across a John Wayne movie and decided to watch it. Before the moving was half over they found themselves back in the bedroom.

While everything seemed to be going well Major Gillis had read all of the reports on Michael that he could. He had studied all of Colonel Dillard's personal notes. He had also been fallowing the news reports on his TV fallowing the beast around the country. He noticed that some people called the creature the beast while others called it the Neanderthal. It did look like a large Neanderthal but the name "beast" came from Doctor Reilly in one of Colonel Dillard's reports. He also noticed that the Neanderthal had been moving around the country a great deal making it look like it, or someone was trying to show it all over the place. Gillie knew that this was the actions of someone that might be trying to lead him away from the real beast. This also left Gillis with no idea where the beast, Michael, or Evie could be.

Under the advise of Colonel Dillard; Gillis continued to used Lieutenant Piles. One day Gillis called Piles into his office. After talking with him for a few hours he placed the Lieutenant in charge of finding Michael and Evie. He offered a company of soldiers but Piles wanted a small team using only five soldiers. He would pick the soldiers. Piles would take his small team into the area where Michael and Evie were last thought to be.

Two days later Piles had chosen five soldiers; two of which were also from Army Intelligence. The next day they left for the area around an old home that belong to a Dan Briks. That was where Michael and Evie were believed to have been last.

Piles and his group got two motel rooms to operate out of in a small town only about five miles from Briks' home. That night Piles and his group went to a local restaurant to eat a nice meal before starting work in the morning. As they sat around a large round table Piles looked over to his right and saw a familiar face. It was Colonel Briks and a woman.

There was one thing that bothered Piles about Briks. What was he a Colonel of? He knew that he had to find out. He called

Sergeant Bails and had him check out Briks. He wanted to know everything about the man.

Major Gillis was not like Colonel Dillard. He did not involved Bails in everything. Because of this Bails never had anything to call Michael or Briks about. But when he got the message to check out Briks he had a very good reason to call them both.

"Don Briks." the Colonel said answering his cell phone.

Bails told Briks about the search that he was suppose to do on him. As Briks talked he looked around and saw someone that he recognized. He saw Lieutenant Piles looking right at him but pretended not to notice him.

"Did he send Lieutenant Piles out here?" Briks asked.

"I don't know." Bails said. "Gillis doesn't tell me things like Dillard did."

"Well he's out here watching me right now." Briks advised.

Briks and Bails finished their conversation and hung up. When Briks and Sandy finished their meal he advised her that they needed to leave. He told her that he would explain in a few minutes. As they drove back to Michael and Evie's home Briks told Sandy about Lieutenant piles. He was worried that she would not want to go out again because of the possible dangers but the situation was actually exciting to her.

Briks would send information to Bails that night to give to Major Gillis. Of course the information would say nothing about God's Soldiers. The rest of the information would be true as Gillis probably already knew that much about him anyway.

Chapter 15

Michael is Missing

As soon as Briks and Sandy got to Michael and Evie's home they went inside where Briks told them about seeing Lieutenant piles. He also told them about Bails calling him. Then he kissed Sandy and left. He had a report to get to Bails.

Michael had stopped carrying his pistol around the property but he started again that night. He was getting very tired of being chased and hounded. He started talking to Briks about him doing something to end this.

Briks was also getting tired of this constant harassment. He had been helping Michael and Evie free of any charges because they were his friends. But when he got home he had to consider another job offer for God's Soldiers.

This job would finish making Briks a very wealthy man. It was his dream to continue running God's Soldiers from home sending his people to do jobs without him. He was getting older and was starting to feel it.

The next morning Briks came back to see Sandy. He had to tell her, Michael, and Evie about this last job. After giving Sandy a big hug he climbed into his truck and left. He had a great deal of work to do before God's Soldiers could leave for the job. When he drove away Sandy started crying.

Evie walked Sandy back to the kitchen table and they sat down to talk. Michael just sat there quietly and let them talk. Finally he went to bed. About an hour later Evie joined him.

Everything seemed to be going well until one day Michael noticed a black van sitting out on the road. He got his binoculars and looked at the van and noticed that two people sat in it and they were watching him. Then he got his M-14 rifle with a 12 x 46 scope on it. He raised it in plane view of who ever was watching him and took aim. He had no intentions on firing at them but they still got the message. The van cranked up and quickly left.

"What'cha shooting at?" Evie asked.

"A black van." Michael told her. "Someone was watching us."

Evie told Sandy and Jane so they could keep watching. Jane was a loyal friend but she was starting to get scared. She even talked to Evie about quitting and moving on. Two days later Sandy spotted the black van again and it was all Jane could take. She talked to Evie and Sandy and then quit.

Jane got her things together and put it all in the truck. Michael would run her into town to her aunt's home. She wanted to stay close because they all had become friends.

When Michael pulled the truck around the home he stopped. This time the black van was sitting on the road just feet from their driveway. He pulled his pistol and lay it in his lap. Jane started shaking. Then he slowly drove out onto the road and right up against the van. Only a few feet from the driver in the van he smiled at the driver.

"You looking for someone?" Michael asked the driver. He noticed two other men in the van as well.

"We're surveyors Sir." the driver said. "We aren't watching anyone."

"Surveyors work out in the field and you three never get out of the van." Michael advised. Then he pointed his pistol at the driver. "If I see this van again ... or any other vehicles sitting out here I'm gon'a open fire with my rifle." He lowered his pistol and added; "Okay?"

"Yes Sir." the driver said and cranked up the van. As Michael drove away the van did as well.

Michael took Jane to her aunt's home and helped carry her things inside. Before leaving he looked up and saw the black van two blocks away watching him. When he left he drove towards the van which left before he got to it. He was trying to calm down and not seeing the van again helped. He drove on home.

"I think things are coming to a head Babe." Michael told

Evie as he walked in the home. Then he told her about the black van.

"And Briks will not be back for two weeks." Evie added.

"Just keep the doors locked and start carrying your pistol." Michael advised.

"I have a pistol and a box of ammo." Sandy said. "Would you care if I also carried?"

"I have no problem with it." Michael assured her.

Back at Jane's aunt's home there was a knock on the front door. When Jane answered the door she saw two police officers standing there.

"My I speak to Jane Wilson?" the bigger officer asked.

"That's me but ... what did I do?" Jane asked."

"We have a warrant for your arrest ma'am."

Jane knew that something was wrong. She did nothing illegal. "What did I do?"

"We will explain everything down at the station ma'am." the shorter officer added as he grabbed Jane's upper arm. The other officer grabbed her other arm and they walked her outside.

Jane knew that something was wrong. The police always handcuffed a person they were taking in and she was not handcuffed. When they walked up to the car she noticed that the car was not from the local police department. The side of the car only said the word "POLICE." She stopped only to be thrown into the car and taken away.

Michael saw a bag on the floor that belonged to Jane. He tossed it in the truck and quickly drove to her aunt's home to take it to her. That was when Jane's aunt told him what had happened. Michael quickly got back home.

Michael told Evie and Sandy what had happened and then quickly started adding things to his book.

From the Author's Wife

My husband wrote almost all of this novel but I have had to add a few things. Government men came into our home without knocking and took Michael away. Then I was threatened and told that if I mentioned that this story was true or that they were even there I would simply come up missing; like him. That was three years ago and I still have not seen or heard from my husband. But, I have had enough and decided to finish and publish his book; this book.

I apologize for how this novel ended but that was when the government forced their way in. Over the past three years I have added a few things to it but decided to leave it unfinished; as my husband left it when he was kidnapped.

I published this book as a fiction novel because no publisher would publish it as a true story. Three times publishers started to publish this as a nonfiction book only to have the government threaten them. But published as a fiction novel the government did not seem to mind.

Soldiers rushed into our home and shot Michael with a dart gun drugging him to the point that he was out cold. Then they carried him away. They did not seem to care about me our our unborn child.

So now we must go on the run after publishing this novel and especially after adding this letter to my husband's novel. You can trust the government if you want. They do their testing of many things on our veterans and children. This story really is true whether you believe it or not. Poison kills whether you believe it or not. Our government is a poison and you are nothing to them but a lab rat. Trust me. I know.

Now I and our little girl must go on the run and hide the best we can. I have got to keep getting the news out there and this letter is just one attempt to do that. You are nothing but a lab rat to your government. Remember that.

This is not a novel but a true story. I know. I lived it with him.
Evelyn Reilly Gibbins

Other Publications of

Vernon Gillen

Below is a list of my other novels and books that have been published.

Novels

1. "Texas Under Siege 1."
Tale of a Survival Group Leader.
After a man is voted as the leader of his survival group in Texas a self proclaimed Marxist president asked the United Nations troops to come in and settle down the civil unrest. The civil unrest was really nothing but Americans that complained about how he ran the country.

2. "Texas Under Siege 2."
The Coming Storms.
The young group leader continues to fight when the countries that made up the United Nations troops in the United States decided to take over parts of the country for their own country's to control.

3. "Texas Under Siege 3."
The Necro Mortorses Virus.
As the group leader continues to fight the UN he learns that an old organization really controlled everything. They were known as the Bilderbergs. Tired of the resistance in Texas they release the Necro Mortorses virus also known as the zombie virus.

4. "Texas Under Siege 4."
250 Years Later.
This novel jumps 250 years into the future where the Bilderbergs are still living with modern technology while the other people have been reduced to living like the American Indians of the early 1800's. One of these young man stands up

and fights the Bilderbergs with simples pears and arrows.

5. The Mountain Ghost 2."
    The Legend Continues.
    The Mountain Ghost continues to fight the Chinese and North Koreans soldiers that have invaded the entire southern half of the United States.

6. "The Mountain Ghost 4."
    The Ghost Warriors.
    After Russ and June have twin girls they grow up and move back south to fight the Chinese and North Koreans as the Ghost Twins. Before long they grow in numbers and call themselves the Ghost Warriors.

7. "Neanderthal."
    As a child he was injected with alien DNA. While in the Navy he was injected with Neanderthal DNA. Now because of these two injection without his knowing young Michael Gibbins changes into a six and a half foot tall Neanderthal from time to time. He grew up being bullied in school and wished that he could change into a monster so he could get back at them. Now he wishes he could take that wish back.

Other Books

1. "Carnivores of Modern Day Texas."
    A study of the animals in Texas that will not only kill you but in most cases will eat you.

2. "Zombies; According to Bubba"
    After studying the Necro Mortises virus for my novel *Texas Under Siege 3*, I realized that I had a great deal of information on it. After finishing the novel I wrote this book leaving the reader to make their own decision.

Unpublished

A great deal goes into publishing a novel or book that takes time. After I write a novel I have someone proofread it. Then I have to find an artist to draw the cover picture which is hard to do. Actually finding an artist is easy but finding one that I can afford is not so easy. Then the novel or book has to be approved by the publishing company. Only then is it published. Then you have kindle and that opens another can of worms.

The fallowing novels are unpublished as I write this but will be published soon. Keep checking Amazom.com for any new novels that I have published.

1. "The Mountain Ghost 1."
   The Legend of Russell Blake.
   After the Chinese and North Koreans attack the southern United States two young brothers, Brandon and Russell Blake go after the invading enemy. After Brandon is killed Russell smears a white past allover his exposed skin and earns the name Mountain Ghost.

3. "The Mountain Ghost 3."
   The Ghost Soldiers.
   After the death of Russell Black his son, Russ, continues as to bring death and destruction to the enemy as the new Mountain Ghost.

5. "The Glassy War."
   Three thousand years in the future and three galaxies away the United Planet Counsel fight and enemy that is trying to control every galaxy they come to. After both starships crash into the planet the survivors continue to fight.

6. "The Fire Dancers."
   I stopped writing this novel to start writing the Mountain Ghost series but I will be getting back to it.

I hope that you have enjoyed this novel. Please help me by sending your comments on what you thought about this novel or book by e-mailing me at <u>bubbasbooks@msn.com</u> . By doing this you will help me to be a better writer. You will also let me know what you, the public, is looking for in these types of novels and books. I have a very creative mind, a bit warped some say but, still creative but, I still need to know what you are looking for. I thank you for your assistance in this.

Vernon Gillen

Made in the USA
Columbia, SC
16 November 2022

71047654R00091